JUST ANOTHER CUBAN

Silvia C. Rodríguez

Just Another Cuban
Copyright © 2016, Silvia C. Rodríguez
Cover illustration © 2015, Diana Calderón
Translation: Edward Sadar
English editor: Pamela Bayer

ISBN-10: 1-63065-047-1
ISBN-13: 978-1-63065-047-6

PUKIYARI PUBLISHERS
www.pukiyari.com

With thanks:

*To God, for all of the blessings
he grants to me daily.
To my husband, Goose Rodríguez, for the
unconditional support that he offered during the
writing and publishing of this book, and always.
A special thanks to a great Cuban, whose tenacity
on the face of almost unsurmountable struggles
became my inspiration. Thank you, Roberto.
To my publisher, Ani Palacios and her team at
Pukiyari, for their professionalism and advice.
Thanks to my talented niece, Diana Calderón, for
the beautiful piece of art which she painted
especially for this book.
To my dear friend Edward Sadar for translating
this book. I appreciate the dedication
and fine work he did for me.
Thank you to my English editor Pamela Bayer.
To my parents, Miguel Carrillo and Silvia
Escudero; my brother, Cesar Carrillo, for their
encouragement and constant support.
A special thanks to my friend Sharon Stanfield for
her collaboration in the editing of this book.
To all of you, my gratitude, from the bottom
of my heart*

I dedicate this book to all the Cubans, as well as all immigrants of other nationalities, who emigrate to the United States of America in search of a better life.

Chapter One
My Birth

She is a beautiful young woman at the early age of sixteen, filled with innocence and all her life ahead of her when she meets the love of her life…

***

It is barely eight in the morning, a sunny day in the middle of the week, when she arrives at the hospital for her check-up. The man by her side is supposingly her great love. Already dressed in a small white robe, made of rough fabric and impregnated with the traditional smell of a clinic, she waits patiently in the examining room. The doctor, tall, dark, and thin, finally enters. He's a serious gentleman of few words. After a rushed greeting, he gears his attention to the file that sits on an old desk. He takes a stethoscope from its hook on the wall and places the file to one side. At the same time, a nurse knocks on the door and asks for permission to enter the examining room. Without making eye contact with the teenager, the polite nurse greets the doctor by saying, "Good morning" and makes a stiff gesture, as if wanting to smile. She immediately turns to the doctor, "The injection is ready, doctor."

"Very good. The vital signs are normal; all appears to be in order. One moment please," the doctor responds, slowly sliding his hands into his vinyl gloves.

The young girl, confused and afraid, feels her heart rate racing more and more. She asks with a nervous voice, "Doctor, what are you going to do to me?"

The doctor raises one eyebrow and with an expression of surprise, responds, "You don't know why you are here?" Slowly approaching the exam table, he explains, "We're going to interrupt your pregnancy."

She screams with terror and despair. "No, doctor, please no! I'm four months pregnant!"

The young woman leaps out of bed and pushes the nurse, sending the syringe flying from her hands. She runs as fast as she can, her eyes filled with tears.

A short period passes, five months to be exact. On the tenth of November, 1972, I was born.

I came into this world in a province of Cuba called Granma and the city, Bayamo, where the National Anthem of my country was written. It was my bad fortune that I never had the opportunity to know this place because my mother and father were separated a short time after I arrived into this world.

In school, I became fascinated as I learned the history of my birth city. I imagined what life was like in 1513, when the city of Bayamo was founded inland to avoid the attacks of the pirates. I thought about the famous role that the village had in the fight for Independence. It was the first city taken by the rebels and their leader, Carlos Manuel de Céspedes. I envisioned myself in the Church of San Salvador, where a devotee first performed the march which became our National Anthem in support of the Guerillas of Indepence.

My mother moved with me to the city of Guantánamo and my father went to live in Havana. They took separate paths, so I did not have much contact with my father or his family, and I never met my paternal grandparents.

My mother showed up at her family's home in Guantánamo with me in her arms. Through the stories which I would hear later, I deduced that I was only two months old. Arriving without warning and carrying me close to her bosom, naturally my mother encountered problems with her family but fortunately, in the end, we were accepted.

***

It is here—"as a Son of the Revolution"—that the first years of my life began in the city of Guantánamo where I was raised. The location remains in a rural, hot, and somewhat humid zone between mountains with dense vegetation but with a mild and enjoyable climate.

I loved it when it rained there. In those times, I would sit and listen to the water strike against the windows. Sometimes, I would to go out to the porch and sit in an old, noisy, rocking chair to enjoy the aroma of the wet earth; it relaxed me. The best was when the hail would fall. I would look upwards and ask myself: *Where is the ice coming from?* It simply and suddenly appeared. I observed it falling in the countryside, bouncing when it touched the ground. The ice suddenly appeared and I saw it falling in the countryside, bouncing when it touched the ground. At times, I imagined that they were little icemen that came from another planet and landed outside to invade Earth. I would remain very quiet, watching until the ice stopped falling. Little by little the ice melted away as it was touched by the rain, disappearing at the same time as my fantasies.

Our family had a farm with a house of traditional Spaniard construction and the surroundings were beautiful. I remember that there were large sugar cane plants, much fruit, and birds of all different sizes and colors that awakened us each morning with all kinds of songs. There was also lush and colorful vegetation and passionfruit trees with their yellow flowers adorning the stony streets of the village. Nature was exuberant in Guantánamo. The village was a coffee bean producing center, which was the principal source of income of the inhabitants. There were many Spaniard families, most of which were owners of the coffee plantations.

I was born with the Cuban Revolution; my oldest memories date from, more or less, age four.

To make it to my grandmother's house, I had to go down a road of about five kilometers. In those times there were no highways but only dirt tracks over which horses, mules and oxen traveled. My grandmother's house sat at the end of a dusty path. It was a little sky-blue farmhouse, with a red-tiled roof. The house was surrounded by flowers of all colors and fruit bushes. My grandmother loved to plant guava, oranges, mamey, guiro and many other fruits.

I remember that my family's house had a concrete patio where we dried the coffee. There, among the dark fragrant beans, we played all afternoon.

Near the house was a river in which we swam among the little fish. I, always unsuccessfully, would try to capture them with my hands. We had a lot of freedom in those days. I played with an uncle, my mamá's brother, named Alejandro. He was only two years older than me. I also played with an aunt who was only four years older than myself. My grandmother had thirteen children, so the house was always filled with family but there were also many kids in the neighborhood; we played and played with them for most of the day. We liked to hunt birds with arrows or slingshots. We would go to the outskirts of town in search of fruit. We played with "balinas or bolas", as we called the marbles. We also liked to play "hopscotch", a game in which one paints numbers on the ground and then throws pieces of metal at the numbers; it was all so much fun.

Clearly, it was not all recreation; at home, we were given chores to do. Bringing water from the river is a traditional responsibility of the children in my village. Very early in the morning we walked some 250 meters to arrive at the river, fill the tanks with water, and carry the heavy weights home. The river was very clear and the water so transparent. Thinking of those days, brings back very beautiful memories. The water that we, the children, carried was used for everything at home: to drink, to wash, to bathe.

My grandmother made us breakfast and always called us back from play at about midday for lunch. My grandmother could really scream! We could hear here from a kilometer away and in her strong voice she would call, "Lunchtime!" and we came running filled with enthusiam for grandma's cooking. Ah! The exquisite meals of my grandmother, how could I forget! Afterwards, we would returned to our childish games and adventures. In those times we lived with much freedom. In the early evening, our grandmother would scream again and we dined as a family. We enjoyed the delicious casseroles that she prepared. Later in the evening, we continued to play, perhaps tag or hide-and-seek. Those times of frolicking did not last long. I turned five and started school and was given new responsiblities. In addition to studying, I was sent on errands for food supplies. I also helped with some household chores. Generally, life in the country was very wholesome.

***

Time moves on and my mamá meets a new man and decides to start her life over; that man would end up being the father to my sister, Karen. My mother then goes to live with him in another province near Guantánamo, in a little village called Mayarí Riva. She moves me with her. In this village, my mother builds one of the most beautiful houses. It has two stories, one bathroom, a kitchen and a living room. It's a simple country house but very comfortable, made of fairly strong wood. In Mayari, life is normal and it was there that my sister, Karen, was born. Sometimes, at the age of five, I took care of Karen so that my mamá could go to work. I attended a small school and when I returned home in the afternoon, I stayed with my baby sister. We lived there for about two years, until my mother left my step-father because he had another relationship. My mother would not tolerate his infidelity. Poor mamá; it was another blow to her love life.

My mother, disappointed, sold the house and we moved to another city in the East of Cuba, a village called San Germán in the province of Holguin. There, the Soviet Union built an immense sugar warehouse. My mamá bought a small house. I remember the house costing two thousand Cuban pesos, which would not even buy a bike today, but we had everything that we needed. My life went on normally, like any other child of the same age. I atended school and had friends. We almost always played the same games: marbles, spinning tops, kites. We had a movie theater and parks for entertainment. The village also had the Carnivals of San Germán, where one could meet with villagers in the main street. It was a great party where the crowd danced, ate and drank prior to the holy time of Lent. We lived quietly with a house, humble and modest, and thanks to my mother's hard work, we never lacked food on the table. We were happy and lived there for three years.

Chapter Two
My Father Shows Up

A few years flew by, I was already in elementary school, and had no idea about my father. He was never mentioned at home, photos of him were never around and I never asked about him. Simply, for me, the word "papá" did not exist.

One fine day in San Germán, I was eight years old and my father appeared.

***

It is a Saturday afternoon. I am playing on the patio, when I hear my mamá calling me from the living room of our house, "Ernestico! Come here, I have to introduce you to someone!" I perceive that the tone of my mamá's voice is strange; there is something different about it that intrigues me. As I am running to her, the first thing that I notice is a strange gentleman standing by her. He has a light complexion and is well-built; and with his light-colored eyes, he looks at me with curiosity but seriousness. My mamá says softly, "He is your father. He came all the way from Havana."

I remain standing in the entrance to the living room, not knowing what to do or think. In an instant, something pops into my mind and goes through my soul. I feel my heart beating harder and for the first time in my life, I know that he exists. My father exists and is here in front of me. I want to run toward that man and hug him, but I can't! He is a stranger to me; I'm paralyzed.

Finally, I breathe out, "Oh, my papá!" I say nothing else. Approaching me slowly, with a certain shyness and great emotion he says to me, "Ernesto, son, I brought you this." He shows me a package. I see some clothes, a pair of shoes and many candies, even better, caramels! I scream from within: *How nice is my father! He brought me all these things from Havana! My dad is the best!* The emotion, locked in my body, does not know where to escape.

That day, I spend time with my dad and we chat for a couple of hours. I tell him about my school and my favorite games. I realize that my father is a happy person, and that makes me happy, but then he leaves. He is on his way to Bayamo, a city in the province of Granma, his original destination. On his way to Bayamo, he had decided to take a detour to see me, or better said, to meet me.

My father says goodbye, takes the train to his final destination and I'm left with my presents, my sweets and the memory of the few hours that we spent together. It all seems like a dream, as if it hadn't happened at all.

***

"Ernestico, what is going on with you? These days you have been unbearable! Why are you behaving so badly? Come, sit down, we are going to eat dinner."

"I don't want to eat; I don't like it!" I say, and in a rage, I throw my dish. I challenge my mom on everything. Every daily task, including the most insignificant ones, becomes a problem for me. I behave terribly toward my mamá.

"What has gotten into you?! Why are you behaving so badly? That's it! No more games until you behave yourself. You're being punished!"

I leave, run to my room and throw myself on my bed; I feel a great emptiness in my chest and I explode in tears. *What is happening to me? Why can't I stop crying? I want to run outside and never stop. I want to tear this house to pieces, grrrrrr! I just… I just want my father! Why did he go? Why did he leave me?* I don't understand; I scream in silence, feeling a pain that runs through my whole body and I don't know how to calm it. The hours go by, the night is long, and it's as if time had stopped or slowed with creeping hopelessness. Now, exhausted, sleep finally defeats me and I pass out.

I open my eyes and it is already another day. I manage to see the rays of the sun that enter through the window and know that it will be a sunny day. The air feels hot but I feel that I have no energy. I don't want to get out of bed. I don't have the energy to begin the day with my normal enthusiasm, ready to go to school. Today, I can't; the only thing going through my mind is my father. I am sad, confused and at the same time, filled with rage.

I hear my mother preparing breakfast in the kitchen, the smell of coffee wafting into my room. I ignore it and roll over in bed.

"Ernesto, get up, it is time to go to school!" yells my mamá while continuing her work in the kitchen. I curl up again between the sheets, opting not to answer.

"Ernesto, I know that you're awake and I am not going to tell you twice; get ready quickly! You have school!"

"I am not going to school!" I yell exasperated. There is silence; I don't hear the sound of the kitchen anymore.

"Yes, you are. I don't care if you are awake with a bad attitude, you can't stay here all day," my mamá states, with calm determination.

"I don't want to go! I am not going! No, No!"

I run to where she is and finally I am able to yell with all of my strength, "I want my dad! My dad was really great! You're not, you don't even love me!"

I run back to my room and throw myself on the bed but I cannot stop crying until fatigue defeats me and I fall asleep again.

"Ernesto, son, it's been hours. Get up. Your clothes are ready. We are getting on the train this afternoon because we are going to Bayamo. We are going to search for your dad."

Chapter Three
Life With My Father

That was the biggest mistake I made in my life. I never should have left my mother. My mamá gave me the opportunity to know my father and I should have been thankful. She had always done enough for me. She went through life alone, fighting against wind and high water.

My problem began about two days after arriving in Bayamo, the place where I found my father.

***

My father went to look for me where my mother told him to meet me. She says her good-byes to me with a kiss, a hug and a couple of recommendations. Immersed in my own childish thoughts, it doesn't occur to me in that moment that my mother's heart is breaking into thousands of pieces. Moments later, my father and I leave to take a bus and in a few minutes arrive at the train station.

"Follow me, and don't leave my side," he indicates without an explanation. We enter the station and go to the travel information board for local trains. My father stops, reads everything there, focuses on finding the hours of departure, the train number and destinations.

"Two tickets for Havana," he directs the clerk while he pays him the money.

Oh! We're going to Havana, I've never been there!

I am excited that we are going to Havana. It is a new experience with my father; I don't want to miss even the smallest detail. The counter is high. Standing on my tiptoes, I barely reach to see the man preparing two tickets and asking our names. While my father answers him, I closely observe how the clerk writes the information on a rectangular piece of paper, next to the printed orange letters and when he finishes, he proceeds to hand the boarding passes to my father.

My father leads me toward a door that opens in the back part of the building towards the train tracks and I follow him in silence.

I don't know how much time has passed but to me it is like an eternity. I am bored, trying to entertain myself walking from side to side, playing with sticks and putting my ear on the tracks to see if I can manage to detect the train approaching. I finally see the train and hear its whistle. The closer it gets, the more I can see it's huge size. It's immense! The noisy locomotive passes right in front of us and the clatter of the trains' wheels on the tracks disappear the moment it stops. My father, with the tickets in hand, leads us on board. After walking through a couple of cars, we find two empty seats.

"Go on, Ernesto, sit on that side, these are ours," my father points and I obediently sit next to the window. All of the train windows are open because it's hot inside but as soon as the train begins to move, I feel a refreshing breeze. This is how the new stage of my life begins.

The trip is long; it seems too slow. To curb my boredom, I kneel on the vinyl seat, turn my head downwards and look out the train window. The glass is opaque and dirty, the metal sides of the train are scratched and parts of it are rusted. I raise my sight toward the horizon where I can see mountains in the distance. We pass through spectacular valleys, fields planted with sugar cane and coffee beans, and occasionally I saw animals: goats, pasturing cows, oxen plowing the fields. We also pass through populated areas, especially when we were near train stations. In many of the cities, the buildings I see have peeled paint up and down along their exterior walls. I believe that those houses would be prettier if they gave them a fresh coat of paint. Never before had I paid attention to all these things as I do now. The little patios of the houses, sit next to the train tracks. Some are enclosed with wood and others with mesh. There were clothes hanging in the sun and a variety of plants. I believe that they're banana trees or palm trees; there are so many bushes that I could not name them all. I asked myself what kind of animals would live here, *perhaps hutias, toads, and bats?* Immediately, I could see myself playing among the leaves, inventing adventures of exploration.

I lose myself in my imagination until I realize that the train has stopped moving. We've finally arrived in Havana, Cuba's capital city. The minute that I step of the train, I am aware that it's now a fact; I have left my mother. There's no turning back.

Havana is truly gigantic. I've never seen buildings so large or so close together; some even have balconies with iron railings. I noticed that the iron railings are where the people hang their clothes. The buildings have tall windows with arches at the top; everything is so impressive. The houses are of many colors: pastels of white, pink, blue and yellow. There is a building which especially captures my attention. It is enormous and occupies a city block. It's white and has a series of columns supporting a dome. In the façade the word "Capital" is written. "Capital" must be the name of this spectacular edifice. *Wow, how beautiful is Havana!* There are many poles with wires on both sides, the streets are grand and there are so many cars! I've heard that various car models are made in Russia. There are also many, many people walking through the streets and others traveling on bicycles.

***

Never would I have imagined that my arrival in Havana would have unleashed such a personal struggle. It was a very difficult time. A child does not know what the absence of a mamá means until one lives in that moment and quickly realizes what's the future is going to look like.

Once settled in my father and his wife's house, after two or three weeks have passed, I began to miss my mamá terribly, and yes… the stay with my father is not what I expected.

"It's bed time," my father told me one evening.

I go out to the patio where there's still sunlight. On the bench, I see my spinning top where I had forgotten it. I approach it, picking it up, and when I begin to wrap the string around the top I cannot resist the temptation… I decide to throw it.

I'll throw it only once and then I am going to sleep. Ah! See how great the top spins; it is one of my best moves. I watch it with pride and then glance to the side and see that my new friends approach me. They look intrigued.

"Brilliant! How did you do that? Think you can do that again?" they challenge me in unison.

"Of course I can! Just watch, I'll throw it again!" I say with a smile of satisfaction. While I am wrapping the cord around the old top, I suddenly feel that I have to go to the bathroom. *I really have to pee, but if I go inside, they will not let me play anymore since my dad wants me to go to bed.*

"Wait, I have to go to the bathroom, I'll be right back," I explain and rush to the back part of the patio. Behind the brambles I see some bushes. *Yes, I can do it here; it is a good place to...* I feel hot and wet. *Oh, no! I've wet the bed! Once again, no!*

***

The first few times that I wet myself, my father overlooked this type of distressing event and gave me instructions about what I should do.

"Ernesto, you can't do that. You have to urinate before going to bed. Afterwards, you just have to hold it, or simply get up and go to the bathroom. You're not a baby any more, you know."

Nevertheless, the accidents (or according to my father…"incidents") recurred. He warned me, each time more annoyed and I unsuccessfully promised him repeatedly, "Yes, daddy. I won't do it again; truly I won't do it again."

Over time, these accidents became more annoying and my dad wanted to cure the problem that I had once and for all.

"Oh, no! Again! I've wet the bed!" I grumbled and looked at the old clock that stood on the table next to my bed. It's around two o'clock in the morning; perhaps the mattress will dry out before dawn arrives. I try to take off the sheets to air them out; I cannot sleep. I sit on the edge of the bed, terrified, praying that the sheets will be dry before…

"You did it again?! I told you not to do that. How many times do I have to repeat myself? You're a filthy child. Now you'll see how I'm going to cure your problem!"

I feel a strong tug on my arm that shakes my head and, without knowing how it happened, I suddenly find myself against the wall. I hear how he slams the door with rage. I shudder at the sound… I have goosebumps from head to toe. I realize that I am in trouble, yes, I know that I have a big problem. I am afraid; I feel alone in this little cold room… *Ah! My body is on fire!* It is as if fire travels intensely over every centimeter of my body. *Oh! I am in pain! This torment does not stop!*

"Let's see if you finally understand!" my father screams frenetically. I hear the sound of the leather belt raging and striking my skin over and over. I hear screams filled with rage.

"You are filthy! You'll understand now!"

And that leather belt continues roaring and bouncing with each blow. *This is a nightmare. It has to be a nightmare! But it doesn't stop! I can't escape from it! There is no one to come to my aid! Stop! Please stop daddy, stop! I won't do it again!* I want to scream with all my strength but the only thing that comes out of me are tears. I'm unable to talk. My heart bounces in my chest and my legs tremble, yet at the same time, I am scared and paralyzed. There is too much pain… terror takes over me… I feel as if I'll faint.

Another day goes by and it's time to sleep but I don't want to go to bed because I am so afraid. The fear and lack of sleep are getting worse each time that it's bedtime. The fear is overwhelming and it transforms into panic and grows with those whipping sessions that persist day after day.

***

There, in that little room, I was so overcome with fearful emotions. It made me feel like a cowering animal looking for an escape. I felt real savagery in that place, in my father's house.

"You're going to wash those sheets right now and you better leave them very clean. Let's see if you've learned."

In the afternoon, my father made me wash the sheets.

"Yes, daddy, I've already washed them."

I washed them in a washbowl with water and a bar of soap, and at the end, my father's wife helped me a little. My stepmother never agreed with my father's methods. She never liked the ways in which he taught me; but at home, one did what the man said… period.

I attended school… I believe that I finished the third or second grade… I don't remember very well. The environment was not as strict as at home but in elementary school I began to have problems. They made me take a special class for children with mental retardation or learning problems. It was because I didn't understand the subjects.

The name of my neighbor was Sigmundo. He would take his wife, his son and me to school every morning because he was one of the privileged few who could say that his family owned an automobile. I liked riding with them in the car. That hour of driving to school was the only moment of the day that I enjoyed. Sigmundo's wife, Irma, came with us because she worked in the kitchen of the elementary school.

In school, they fed us lunch and a snack, as the classes began each morning and ended each afternoon. I still fondly remember the school cafeteria, which was one of the stable things in my life.

My ability to learn became more and more deficient. I lived as if I was in a catatonic state. I started attending school with bruises all over my body. My father now started hitting me in the head. He was hitting me everywhere.

"Ernesto, will you tell me what is happening to you? You can talk to me, I am your teacher and you can confide in me. What happened to you? Why are you so bruised and scarred?" Filled with worry, the young lady asked me such questions over and over. I was unable to respond; it was as if I were paralyzed. I simply could not speak.

The young teacher advised the school of my situation and they gave her the task of finding out where I lived. She discovered that Irma, the school cook, was my neighbor and asked her if she knew what was happening to me. She said, "Oh no! It's horrible; they beat that child every morning!" The school officials investigated further and they learned more details about my situation and with whom I lived… the whole mess. They learned that my mamá did not live with me.

My mother continued living in the East of Cuba, while I was in Havana. Apparently, I had an aunt that lived near the school I attended. I didn't have much to do with that aunt because she was the sister of my mamá and my father didn't allow me to visit her. Somehow, the school officials contacted my aunt and obtained my mamá's address.

All of this happened on Thursday. My mamá received the telegram around noon and without making any plans, she immediately went directly to the station and took the train to Havana. She was willing to travel the long ten hour trip.

***

It is Friday. It is four in the afternoon and the school bell sounds, classes have ended. I gather my supplies and put them neatly in my leather backpack — oh, how I hated the straps of that backpack! Each time that I carried it on my back, the straps dug into my shoulders. I walk toward the building's exit. To my surprise, I see my mamá at the entryway. *My mamá is picking me up at school!* I let go of my backpack and run toward her. She hugs me and I hug her, I can feel her warmth. *My mamá! You're here! You came to rescue me!* Relief and tears are in my eyes and I don't want to let her go; not even for a second.

"I am now here, Ernestico, let's get your backpack. I'll help you with it, relax. Now we are going to your aunt's house, son," she whispers and caresses my head with gentleness. Those were the most comforting words I had heard in a very long time.

At about six in the evening, my mamá and I arrive at my father's house. My heart started to pound faster as soon as she knocked on the door. I'm afraid… I'm so very nervous, but when my mamá takes me by the hand I feel more secure.

I hear steps approaching and someone opens the door. Here he is, my father.

"You finally show up; you should have been here hours ago," he speaks to me, ignoring my mother. However, my mamá, not worrying about my father's conduct, remains firmly in the doorway and looks him in the eye.

"I've come to get my son's clothes; I'm taking him with me," she says calmly but in an intense tone. My dad moves slowly in front of her. There is a short but profound silence. I can hear the soles of his shoes touching the concrete floor. He approaches her more closely and responds to her with exasperation:

"No, Ernesto is not moving from this house."

My mother without a hint of fearfulness, tells him, "Did you not hear me tell you that I've come for my son?"

He answers with his voice raised, "You can only take him if he wants to go. If he doesn't want to go with you, he remains here. I'm his father, and right now I'm telling you that Ernesto loves me and he doesn't want to go with you; he has told me this many times."

Anxiety takes over and pressure grows along with worry. *Oh, no! She is going to think that's true! What is going to happen now? What can I do so that my mamá knows that I love her? I have to leave this house right now.*

I'm so afraid of my father, and yes, at times I've told him that I'd never go with my mamá. However, it's because I am terrified of him. In spite of the attitude and words of my father, my mamá doesn't back down. On the contrary, without hesitating, she places her hand on the top of the door, elevates her chin, and with a penetrating look and with her voice filled with rage, says, "My son is coming with me even if I have to kill you, your wife and your daughter! Above all, I'm ready to fight anybody standing in my way! So, the best thing for you to do is to bring his clothes down here and to give them to me, so I can take him home! Do you understand?"

Then my father turns toward me and leans very close to my ear, shaking his head with displeasure and cynically asks me, "You want to go with her?"

I feel his eyes piercing my soul. I am cold and my body trembles; I take refuge behind my mamá. *This is my chance to leave from here, from this place; I have to be courageous and strong if I don't want more mayhem in my life. If I don't want more of this suffering.* And finaly… I dare. Murmuring, almost without a voice, my head bent and my gaze lost in the floor; I can barely pronounce the simple words, "Yes, I want to go with her."

My father gives me two or three items of clothing and I leave with my mother by my side. *Relief at last!* I can breathe deeply because there is a light of hope. *I'm safe, I'm with my mother. I'm not going to be separated from her ever again… how I missed her!*

After all the commotion, we arrive at the house of my mamá's cousin and I am back at the village where I grew up. Such peacefulness, ahhhh!

Chapter Four
Returning With My Mother

In 1982, I was eight years old and arrived in the little village of Cojimar. We settled into a small room with a relative of my grandmother, a dark-skinned woman named Elba. It wasn't the best thing that happened in our life but it was okay. I was with my mamá and my sister, Karen, which was all that was important to me.

I continued to have my bed-wetting problem. My mamá also fought with me; she tussled enough to make me overcome that obstacle. The difference between her and my father is that my mother helped me by having all of the patience in the world. I think that she knew that this was not a problem I was creating to be defiant. Truly, I was not doing it on purpose to cause trouble. No, it was a problem that I could not control and when I least expected it...*boom* (I had an accident). It would always happen when I was sleeping. It was not me; it was my unconsciousness that betrayed me completely.

From the time that I returned to live with my mother, she spent the following year, or perhaps more, trying to cure me. She searched everywhere and found many remedies. We finally won the battle, thanks to the recommendation that was given to my mamá by the Haitian woman. She convinced my mamá of what we had to do and although the method was a little unusual, my mamá actually followed her instructions, step-by step.

***

My mamá is in the kitchen, holding a brick in her hand. It's the kind used in construction, red in color. She places it on top of the black metal kerosene stove's fire to heat it up. From time to time, she lifts the brick with tongs and turns it over until it is red-hot.

"It is now time to go to bed, Ernesto. Let's go outside; the brick is hot enough as it should be."

"Does it have to be now? Just a few minutes more? I am very busy, mamá."

"How busy can you be? You're just playing around! Come, hurry up! The brick is already very hot; we shouldn't wait until it cools, or this remedy will not work."

"Ay, mamá! Please wait for a little moment."

"Not even for one little moment; listen to me, right now!"

"Arrrrr, okay mamá, I am coming, I am coming."

"Follow me, let's go to the patio. You already know that as soon as I put the brick into the ground, you get on your knees and pee on it, understand?"

"But mamá," I whine, "What if I don't have to pee?"

"Did you have the glass of water I left for you on the table?"

"Yes, mamá."

"Then… did you go to the bathroom?"

"Mmmmm, no… yes… but I only went a little."

"Ay, my little boy, you don't pay attention. But you'll figure it out, you'll see. Now, pee on that brick."

"OK, it's all good. I'll try, but if you look at me I won't be able to do it."

My mamá rolls her eyes, crosses her arms and turns her back. I look around to be sure that no one would see me going and then I start to wet the hot brick.

"Mamá, lots of smoke is coming up! It is hot enough!"

"That is how it should be," my mamá responds, eyeing the target.

"Oh, but why did that happen?"

"It's steam, Ernestico, it's going to cure your problem; the heat of the steam will get rid of the chill that you have in your bladder," my mamá explains patiently how the remedy worked, obviously agreeing with the belief of the Haitian.

We meticulously repeated the brick routine for three nights. I never again wet the bed. As incredible as it sounds, the remedy was a total success.

"What a relief, finally, mamá! Mamá, you'll see that I did not wet the bed!"

"How wonderful, my Ernestico. I knew that you would be successful." my mother responds quietly and kisses me on my forehead.

***

During the time we lived in Mrs. Elba's house, I became ill, which complicated things. I could not attend school for three months, during which I stayed in bed. The doctor said that I had an illness called hepatitis. Rest and eating lots of sweets was what he prescribed. Rest was aggravating… but eating sweets? Ahhh! What great medicine that doctor gave me; I liked him a lot.

I love being with my mamá, she takes great care of me. There is nothing better than being with my mamá; she loves so much!

From that moment on, in my short life, I learned to appreciate all that my mother did for me and for my sister. In Cuba, we had education, medical, dental, ophthalmology and everything else that was needed. Furthermore, the services were excellent. Later on, the situation changed, and not for the better.

Things began to stop going well with Elba, my grandmother's cousin, with whom we shared a home. One day without warning she told us rather coldly that we had to leave her house.

"Ernesto, get your suitcase ready. I'll take charge of your sister; we are leaving."

And so it went, we continued our journey, leaving behind yet another home.

I remember that my mamá luckily was able to save about two thousand pesos from selling our house we owned in San Germán, prior to living with Elba.

Again, the search for a new place to live started. My mamá finally found an apartment that consisted of a small room with a bathroom and a kitchen. A woman constructed this space in the back of the patio of her house. Our little apartment, like the majority of housing in Cuba, was cement with a concrete roof and floor. The place was tiny but it was all my mamá could afford.

I remember that we had only been living there for about eight months when the woman who rented it to my mamá wanted to evict us. Fortunately, my mother had much foresight and intelligence when she signed the rental agreement and gave the deposit to the owner. Mamá signed in an addendum to the rental agreement which worked in our favor in Court. With one more success, we got to stay in our little room.

My mother made sure that we never would lack anything. My mother had been a fighter all of her life; I considered her a warrior. She always worked two or three jobs. One job was in a clothing store's office as a bookkeeper. Her workday was nonstop because immediately after her bookkeeper job, she would then go to work in a market where she sold food while additionally doing the accounting, billing and all other office responsibilities. Later, in the afternoons, she'd return home briefly to prepare supper so that we could eat together. But her working day did not end there. In the evening, she used her sewing machine to sew, usually into the early hours of the morning. She told me that dressmaking earned her more money than her work in the office.

One of the many goals of my mother was to extend the small room in which we lived, and she was successful. She built a second floor, practically adding another apartment upstairs. We lived comfortably for four years. In Cuba, it was easy to live with dignity. We lived with a decorated and cozy apartment due to the hard work of my mother. She always worried about feeding us, clothing us and I now know that we received a competitive education.

Since the problems with the landlady continued, my mamá decided to move our home once again.

In Cuba, there is a system in which if someone wants to exchange their house for another, they can request a permission of exchange in a government office. So, as soon as she arranged all of the paperwork, we moved.

My mamá, always searching to improve our housing situation, moved us several times. I lost count of how many times we moved; but in the end, she found a very good apartment. I was nine years old when I started to show interest in sports, especially for kayaking.

Chapter Five
Sports

Walking with my mother one Sunday afternoon, something caught my attention.

"Look, mamá!" I shouted, amazed and pointing to the sea. I tried to show her what had captivated me. "What are you looking at?" answered my mother without stopping.

"I want to practice that sport! I want to do that, mamá, it looks spectacular!"

After much begging and pleading, she briefly stopped walking and glanced over. She sighed quietly and continued with her walking.

"Mamá, mamá, look at that, look out there!" I insisted with desperation while I pulled on her arm and leaned back to try to capture her attention. Finally, she stopped.

"What is it, son?!"

"I would like to do that, please mamá; it would be amazing for me to learn that sport."

"Of course not, Ernestico. Mamá, mamá, mamá. I hear that word a thousand times a day. Son, you know that they practice that sport in the sea; it is very dangerous."

"It isn't if I know how to swim; remember that I went swimming in the river with my cousins."

"What if something happens to you? You could die! Ay no, not even God wants that! Imagine... what would I do if something happened to you? I would die also."

"No mamá... nothing is going to happen to me if nothing happens to them. I assure you nothing will happen to me, I promise you, nothing will happen. Look at how great they go on the open sea! I want to be with them. There's a teacher too! See, he's going with them, mamá... yes?"

That scene would be repeated constantly, and not only when we went walking on the breakwater of the Bay of Cojímar.

There, on the coast of Cojímar, is where I discovered for the first time one of the greatest passions of my life... kayaking.

Cojímar is very pretty or perhaps one should say that it was extremely beautiful. Today one finds it rather destroyed; it's too bad.

I remember those afternoon walks where I was able to enjoy the beauty of the place. One could see plants on all sides of the road... very tall trees with dense outstretched foliage, some with red flowers. There were plants and flowers of different colors everywhere. In addition to the turquoise waters of the Caribbean Sea and its white sands, the village had a lighthouse and a castle tower constructed by the Spaniards on the shore of the sea. The tower was called, "Fuerte de Santa Dorotea de la Luna de la Chorrera" or as it was commonly known, "El Torreón de la Chorrera." The story goes that the ancient castle was built to defend the area. In those days, the one-hundred and thirty-seven inhabitants donated a thousand pieces of Spanish gold, or ducats, for the work which was finished in the middle of 1646 by Governor Álvaro de Luna y Sarmiento because the possibility of an attack by Portugal existed. The village was extremely small with only thirty-seven houses. Much later, in the year 1762, the castle tower was damaged by the canons of the English when King Carlos III of Spain declared war on England. Fortunately, later it was reconstructed.

Nevertheless, beyond the magic of that place, the most important thing for me was that it was where they practiced that sport... kayaking.

Each time we walked along the wharf, with every opportunity, I continued pestering my mother. In truth, I didn't talk of anything, except about kayaking.

***

One day, while walking, my mamá decided to sit on a bench to rest and to contemplate the scenery.

"Look mamá, I like that... I want to do that. Please, let me learn kayaking, please?" I continued insisting while crouching down and bothering a scorpion with a dry branch.

"Oh, Ernesto! What are you doing? See... that insect is going to bite you! Let go of that branch because we are going to leave in a moment."

The words of my mother went through my ears like a flash of lightning. I was so impressed by the kayaking; I was lost in my imagination, thinking that I could be one of those sportsmen.

"If you do well in school, and you behave yourself, perhaps it can be considered."

"Really? I promise you; I am going to behave myself very well and my grades in school are going to be good, you'll see!"

It was not a "yes" from my mother but at least I had made progress.

I was pensive on the walk home, playing with the dry branch I collected earlier and watching those boys rowing and practicing their sport.

"Okay, Ernesto, tomorrow we'll go to see if they still have spots to enroll available," my mamá suddenly surprises me.

"Yes! There are going to be spots available! There have to be… I'm sure!" I reply excitedly and I couldn't stop jumping in joy. *Yeah! A miracle has occurred; I was able to convince my mamá!* That was the most difficult matter; the rest would go well.

That night I could not sleep. I turned over and over in bed, looked at the ceiling, and from time to time turned my head to see if the light of day had finally penetrated through the old curtains. To me, the night seemed very long, almost an eternity. I felt so much emotion.

***

I open my eyes, yawned and while stretching my arms, I remember that this is the day. *Yes! Today is going to be a great day! I need to be ready as soon as possible.* I hurriedly put on my t-shirt and pants without thinking of the hole in my pant leg. I hardly notice that my old and faded pants are becoming increasingly short. I run into the kitchen and find my mamá already preparing breakfast.

"I am already ready, mamá!"

"Ready to do what? Let's go, sit down and have breakfast."

"No, I'm not hungry. Let's go right now, mamá, or they won't have any spots left!" I tell her in desperation.

"Calm down, Ernestico, if it is meant for you, there will be a place. First thing's first… have breakfast."

"Ay, mamá, but…"

She interrupts me, "No buts about it, if you do not eat we are not going anywhere."

With no other option, I sit at the table and my mamá serves me coffee with milk, two pieces of bread and half of a plantain. I devour my meal almost without chewing, trying to lose as little time as possible.

After walking a few blocks and taking a bus, we arrive at the location. Finally! The walk took forever. My mamá moves toward a half-painted metal desk where a young woman is seated; she must be the secretary. Standing almost behind my mother, I listen attentively to her asking for information about the kayaking classes. I, of course, do not want to miss even one detail.

"Here it is, ma'am; you only have to fill out this form and your boy will be enrolled." Those words are music to my ears. *Oh! How great! Now I am going to be able to learn kayaking!* I feel as if I had a knot in my stomach. *How exciting!*

The secretary then takes the form and verifies that it is all correct.

The secretary looks at me, "I suppose that you are Ernestico?"

"Yes, miss," I respond courteously.

"The class starts at eight in the morning; you can come and start tomorrow. You have to be very punctual; at eight you have to be ready to start your class. Bear in mind that the discipline here is very strict."

Nodding my head in agreement I respond to her instructions, "Yes, miss, yes. I'm going to come early enough."

"Just arriving on time is enough," she answers with a smile.

One last day of waiting passes, but this last day comes with the assurance that I have a place reserved for me in the class. With that peace of mind, I will be able to go to bed and sleep more easily.

***

Just as the secretary advised me, I rushed to be on time to practice. I understood that if I arrived late, I would have a problem. Therefore, I arrived on-time and ready (I would actually say "more than ready") for class to begin. I met Pepe, the instructor of kayaking, as soon as I arrived. This was when I began learning the sport.

First, the class consisted of instruction. Afterwards, we recited the class motto and next the instructor would bring the newspaper so that we could read the most important news of the week. This included international news; it was all very educational. After the first part of class, the instructor would take us to warm up along the seashore and then finally, we would train on the kayak.

"Steady, Ernesto, take it easy, don't lose your balance, watch the angle of your arms. Remember, they have to be positioned at more or less ninety degrees," Pepe patiently explained the technique many times to me.

Oh, no! I turned over again! It is not as easy as it appears to be, I thought with desperation each time I fell out. *I didn't even advance one millimeter, ahhh!* Each time my frustration grew more. All my effort didn't make any difference. I felt hopeless… but each time I fell out, I got back in again.

After several days of trying, and thanks to Pepe's patience, I began to progress; first paddling forward a little bit, and then I began to glide a few meters over the water.

Ah! Yes, like this, I'm finally able to navigate this boat! I like this, yes, I really like this a lot! I began to enjoy every second of kayaking. It was an incredible experience to be able to glide over the water.

After a while, I advanced in my training. Later, I was able to row five or even ten kilometers.

At the end of training for the day, I always cleaned my boat and stored it on the kayack wall-rack. Everything had a designated place; all was very organized.

The end of each day, all of our class lined up in a row and one classmate, assigned as the class monitor, recited the class motto which was a phrase written by Cuba's National Poet, Jose Marti."Alone, men don't break like crystal, they die on their feet. Against wind and tide!" We responded as expected. This was how we ended the class each day.

***

My everyday life is rushed. I am always busy. Around ten-thirty in the morning, I am home again. I shower, eat whatever my mother has prepared for me, such as "moros con cristianos", rice and beans, or fried plantains, and then I am off to school.

Classes start at one in the afternoon, therefore, I have to arrive at the elementary school a little before school starts. Fortunately, the school is near my house; walking there is not a problem. I take advantage of walking from my house to school, to reflect on my kayack training.

In the first year I practiced kayaking, it was basically simple learning, a solitary routine without competition. However, the second year, the tournaments began. Pepe decides that I am ready to compete locally and then in other cities. They invite all of the other citys' kayaking teams to participate in the competitions… or at least, that is how a tournament was organized in my days.

All of the boats are lined up along the seashore. I identified my boat, pale yellow with the paint that is a little faded by the sun. As I take my starting position, Pepe was immediately by my side giving me some last minute instructions.

They give the starting sound and I run as fast as I can, dragging my boat to the sea. Once I'm in the water, I board my boat and begin rowing as fast as I can. I start well, paddling strongly, and fixing my gaze forward. *I don't want to look back. I can't lose even a second. I have to go as fast as I can!*

"Let's go, Ernesto! Let's go, let's go! You can do it!" I hear my coach and I know that I can paddle faster and faster.

I can see the finish line! I am here! In the end, I cross gasping for breath and with my heart beating rapidly I listen to the results.

"Ernesto Farías in third place!" The gentleman at the finish line announces my position and the people applaud. The majority of the people are relatives and friends of my competition. Mamá couldn't be there due to her three jobs. Perhaps next time, she'll be able to come and watch me.

And yes, there I ended up in third place. *Ah, how good, I feel satisfied and content.*

"Very good, you did so well, Ernesto." Pepe cheers me on and rewards me with a glass of water.

"Thanks, Pepe. Do you think that I could've done better?" I ask before drinking the water.

"Yes, but don't worry about that now. You're going to see that with constant training, you'll improve your technique and your speed even more, and that's why we are practicing." he tells me while giving me a little pat on my shoulder.

***

Competitions continued throughout the season and I generally placed well.

One day, after training, Pepe asks me if I can wait a moment.

"I have good news, Ernesto."

"Okay, tell me, what is it? What's the news?"

"You have qualified for the National Tournament! I need to advise your mamá that she needs to give you permission to travel to Havana. She'll need to sign some papers."

"Oh! Yes, of course she is going to sign, thank you!"

"We also have to begin more rigorous training; I'll give you the details later."

"Okay, Pepe, thanks. I'm going to try a lot harder!"

"I don't doubt that at all, Ernesto. We'll see each other tomorrow, and don't forget to tell your mamá."

***

The day of the National Competition arrived.

"There are thirty-two boats, Ernesto. I know that you can do it; don't lose your concentration," my coach advised me before the competition.

That was my first experience of not doing well in a kayacking tournament. I remember coming in fifteenth place. *I don't know what happened. Didn't I prepare as I should have? Perhaps, I have to train harder.*

I returned home frustrated, empty-handed, only with the experience of having participated, and above all, having learned that the level of the other competitors was above mine. Ah, but that being said, I returned with the determination and courage to place more effort into my training.

***

Another year goes by and I am now in the seventh grade, practicing hard at kayaking. Kayacking filled me with challenges and satisfactions and I took it so seriously that I dedicated, with great discipline, a lot of time and energy into it.

In 1984, I was finally rewarded for all my strict training when I placed first in the Championship of Havana. In a simple but emotional ceremony, they awarded me a Diploma of Recognition. However, the best part for me was when I heard them say, "Here we have the Regional Champion." It made me feel so proud. Additionally, another small thing was… well, the girls started to hang around me with the help of my new fame. How nice! Yes, in that year things went well… even better than that!

Later, I surpassed the school record for the thirteen and fourteen year old category. That year, they offered me a scholarship that would allow me to have better training. Cuba's government recruits the best talent of all sports and other disciplines in each province, to individually train and prepare for national and international competitions.

Upon accepting the scholarship, I would have to leave home every Sunday night and return every Friday afternoon. It was like an exclusive educational and sports academy specializing in developing my talents.

***

"Ernesto, what's going on? Why don't you want to accept the scholarship?" Pepe asked me in amazement.

"Oh, I don't know." Disheartened, I lower my head without being able to give him an explanation.

"How can you not know? You have a lot of talent; this is a great opportunity for you!"

"Yes, I know," I answered simply and I hid my expression, hoping that the conversation would finally end.

"Just imagine, it's a door that's opening for you. It could be the start of a sports career; it is great for your future and you would even be able to travel!" My coach not understanding my thoughts, tried convincing me a thousand and one different ways.

The sport grabbed my heart; in that moment, it was my great passion. I was also aware that there was better training in that school, better boats, and overall a program much more advanced than the one I have here.

— 58 —

However, accepting that opportunity would mean separating from my mamá once again. The experience with my father, that until now has been burried deep within me, resurges quickly and leaves me confused.

No, never again will I leave my mamá. The fear of what would happen to me emotionally if I left my mother blocks me from taking this next step in the sport.

***

I had made my decision during that conversation with Pepe... or so I thought. I silently repeated the words of my coach all month. I could not stop thinking about the opportunity of growing in the sport and becoming a professional kayaker but the thought of leaving my mother was difficult. The pain of the past stunned me. It took much effort and the encouragement from both my mother and coach, but I finally overcame my insecurities. I changed my mind and asked my mother to accompany me to school. As old as I was, she still had to come with me to authorize any transaction of that magnitude.

"The slots are already filled, Ernesto. Son, they didn't accept you; right now there is no room," my mamá told me with disappointment.

"What? Surely, it's a joke?"

"No, unfortunately, no, it isn't a joke."

Immediately, I was angry and in my arrogance, I could not restrain myself from yelling in rage:

"It can't be, I'm the champion of Havana! What are they thinking? They have to give me the chance!"

I didn't want to believe what I had heard. The government refused to accept me because I made my decision too late and there was nothing that I could do to change the outcome. I decided too late and I could not blame anyone. I was a simpleton, an idiot, a fool!

Filled with frustration and disillusionment, I decided to abandon kayaking. Another mistake I made in my life: I stopped training. Pride won. The arrogance and the impatience of knowing that I would have to wait one more year defeated me.

I tried playing ball for a couple of months but my career as a baseball player was very short. My position was first baseman and during my first game, the ball struck my nose due to my clumsiness. I had no patience for baseball. It bored me and I saw no future in the sport. The reality was that two months is a short time to learn any sport; but more importantly, I understood that the game was not for me and so I quit baseball. Ever since I was a child I never liked team sports; I always leaned toward individual sports.

"Mamá, I have decided that baseball is not for me. From now on, I am going to practice Greco-Roman wrestling," I said, upon entering my house. My mother listened and shook her head in agreement but made a face that showed without a doubt her disapproval… she wasn't convinced, but in the end she supported me all the same.

And so we started the process again, pouring through the applications and all of the mess of signing up, only to discover that my career in Greco-Roman wrestling would last just one month. Similar to baseball, Greco-Roman wrestling was not a good fit for me. Looking back, I attribute my failure to the time when I began practicing this sport. It was winter in Cuba and to me, being used to a hot climate, it was too cold… although it was not as icy as in other parts of the world. I sweated while practicing and afterwards, the drastic temperature change of the cold would give me nosebleeds in the shower.

The doctor explained to my mother that it could be that the training sessions were too difficult but now that I think about it, perhaps it could have been the consequences of that first baseball blow to my nose.

In spite of the fact that I liked the very rigorous training, I decided that Greco-Roman wrestling was not for me either. Every time I practiced, more and more blood gushed from my nose. I had nothing happening. Jumping from one sport to another without finding myself… but, hey, at least I tried.

Chapter Six
An Unexpected Event

When I was finishing the ninth grade, I started to take an interest in a career in athletic training. In order to get more involved in this field, I decided to go to the school's aquatic center. They had a large swimming pool which made it convenient to sign up for swimming classes.

One day, I stayed after swim class to train longer and while practicing, I was interrupted by a conversation between two young animated girls. I neared the edge and stopped to contemplate them. They were chatting and had no idea that I was observing them. I looked at them in detail without paying attention to their conversation. *Such beautiful girls, especially the one on the right, with her light complexion and her slender body.*

Her long dark hair fell over her shoulder as she took off her swim cap. *Oh! What's going on! With that green swimsuit and those long and shapely legs, she looks like a goddess coming down from Olympus. What a beautiful woman!* I asked myself if she would be coming to swim classes every day. *I had never seen her before.* While my interest in a career in athletic training had barely awakened, the attraction I felt for girls had been evident for some time.

The following day, upon returning to my class, I searched, looking far and wide around the swimming pool in hopes of seeing the girls again but I didn't see them anywhere. *Okay, perhaps tomorrow I'll find them here.*

A few days went by and I continued with my routine of attending school and my swimming classes. After a week, I forgot about those girls. *In the end there are a lot more girls,* I encouraged myself, but almost immediately I reflected and understood that realistically it is difficult to meet another girl as beautiful as the one I saw in the aquatic center. *Perhaps I just dreamed of her.*

It is already Friday afternoon; I am yearning to return home to enjoy the weekend a little, and I stress a little because I have a lot of homework to do. At least I don't have to get up early... I slowed down when I suddenly heard a noise. I immediately turned around when a plastic bottle, half-filled with water, rolled down the steps towards me. It was obvious that someone carelessly dropped it. I instinctively bent down to pick up the bottle and as I was picking it up, I was startled to see the beautiful girl that I was admiring a few days ago.

Oh! It really wasn't a dream. It is her; it's the girl from the swimming pool! I excitedly thought while standing up to hand her the bottle.

"Thanks," she shyly said.

"Yes, yes, it's nothing," I answered, stuttering. *This is your chance to meet her, Ernesto,* my inner voice whispered but I couldn't say anything more, and then the other girl joined us.

"Ready?" she asked as her friend approached us.

"Yes, let's go before the bus leaves." She turned to her friend. She gave me a thankful smile for the small act of gallantry.

The two friends started to talk with each other as they walked towards the bus stop while I slowly followed, curiously trying to listen in on their conversation.

"I found out that you were sick; are you better?"

"Yes, it was only a cold and a throat infection but now I am better."

"Are you ready to start training?"

"Yes…"

The further away they got, the more their voices faded, until I couldn't manage to hear their voices anymore and they disappeared from my view.

Ah, but what a fool, Ernesto! You had the chance to meet her, my subconscious screamed at me. Instantly, I made an excuse for myself: *I have too much homework to do, I can't lose much time.*

What an annoyance! Instead of desiring that the weekend would last longer, I was impatient for it to end. *It seems as if the hours were ninety minutes, it's a long weekend; how I wish that it was Monday again.* The odd thing was that something like that had never happened to me before. It was the first time I wanted to return to school as soon as possible… strange, right?

Monday, when classes finally ended, I rushed to the aquatic center knowing that there was a high probability that I would run into that captivating young woman. I decided to try to overcome my shyness and at least try to start a conversation with that beautiful young woman. *Perhaps I can even ask her on a date!* Fantasies took flight in my mind.

Upon arriving at the pool, I saw that she was really there: *the perfect woman.* I could not stop thinking of her during practice. *I need to think up a plan to run into her without seeming obvious.* I couldn't come up with anything. *Think, Ernesto! And if I just approach her when she arrives in class? Mmm, I don't think so; everyone is going to see me, I'll look like a fool... perhaps this isn't a good idea.* The only idea that crossed my desperate mind was when the class ends, I could 'accidently' bump into her, pretending that it was just fate... of course! It would not seem suspicious since she and I left the aquatic center at the same time.

After class, I quickly showered, dressed and rushed to hide in the corridor close to the center's exit. I silently waited to make this meeting happen.

And so it was, we bumped into each other but my fantastic plan did not work out that well; our chat was nothing more than a hello.

Okay, at least I know that she is not avoiding me. She returned my greeting. Once more I made an excuse for things not going exactly my way.

A few days later, I came to the realization that it was going to be difficult for me to ask her out because I had no idea of how to approach her, or to be honest, I did not dare to go near her.

One nice day, I entered the school, hungry and distracted, and I hear someone behind me. Quickly, I turn around to grab the door open as to avoid it swinging into the person's face. *Wait! It's her! She is the one walking behind me, and, just my luck, no one is with her. Will it be destiny?*

"Hello," she greeted me first which I liked because it made me feel more confident.

"Hi, how are you? Did your girlfriend abandoned you?"

"Yes, can you believe it?" She answered with a smile.

"No, of course not."

"Blanca had a family event; so, she couldn't attend today."

"Of course; nice to meet you, I'm Ernesto."

"Yes, I know, I mean, I already knew it, you know… in class..."

What a dummy; how did it occur to me to say that?... arrrrr... I thought to myself; but this time, I continued the chat.

"Yes, right, Yanina?"

"Yes, that's right, my name is Yanina …hahaha," she answered cheerfully.

"If you want, I'll walk with you. Where are you going?"

"Okay, I'm going to my grandmother's house. If you'd like, you can accompany me to the bus stop."

"Give me your gym bag, it looks kind of heavy, I can help you with it."

"Alright, thanks."

"So you live with your grandmother?" It's the first thing that occurred to me to ask.

"No, I am just going to visit her. I live with my mamá. My papá and mamá are divorced; you know…"

"Oh! I understand; my parents are also separated. I live with my mamá too."

"I've always wanted to live with my papá. He is very affectionate with me and we get along very well, but my mamá has never let me do it."

"Not me. I get along very well with my mamá." I preferred not to remember the terrible experience that I had with my father.

We arrived at the bus stop and ended our conversation. It was my bad luck that the bus arrived almost immediately. Anyway, this chat was a good start. Exchanging a few words with Yanina was good enough for me.

A few days went by and nothing important had happened with Yanina. We only greeted each other and talked a little when I walked her to the bus stop.

One afternoon like any other, I came home exhausted; I had finished all of my school activities and sports for the day.

"I'm home, mamá. I'm so hungry!" I yelled just as I entered the house and immediately tossed my gym bag by the doorway.

"First, you are going to hang your bathing suit and towel on the patio; and then, you are going to come here and sit down to eat. Ah! And don't leave your bag thrown there, take it to your room. Boy, you don't ever leave things where they belong."

"Agrrr, but…" I started to protest.

"Listen, don't you think that I get tired?" She interrupts me immediately.

"Agrrr… it's okay, I heard you," I replied making a face. I lazily picked up my backpack, took out the wet clothes and walked slowly out to the patio with my shoulders hanging down, being somewhat dramatic.

"Get going, Ernesto, don't be a martyr; hurry up! I still have clothes to hem today."

I was almost finished hanging my swimsuit on the clothesline when I heard someone call my name; someone was talking to me from the kitchen door.

"Ernesto?"

That voice... I know that voice! I turned and I almost froze when I saw my papá standing there. I was already fourteen years old and much time had passed since the last time I saw my father. Up until that moment, my sister and I had lived peacefully together with my mother in Cojímar.

"Hi, Ernesto," he greeted me with his smooth voice and I just nodded my head.

"I've come to chat with you."

After a short and somewhat uncomfortable silence he continued, "I've come to talk with you about your studies."

I observed my father closely and noticed that there was something different in his appearance. I realized right away that I didn't view him as grand and strong as I used to see him. After a few seconds of processing this fact, I replied, "It's fine; I am almost finished here and I'm on my way."

I went into the kitchen. My mother was standing near the table and on the opposite side, my father was seated.

"Ernestico, your papá came to talk with you for a bit; if you want to sit down, we'll talk while you eat your dinner."

"No, I'm not very hungry anymore." I realized my appetite had actually vanished.

"Come on, sit down. Your mamá also wants to talk with us," my father insisted, making little hand-gestures in the air.

I took the chair closest to my mother and placed my arms on the table. Without realizing it, I distracted myself by observing the tablecloth in detail. *It seems that the red line interlaces with the white ones forming squares of different sizes. I had never before focused on the pattern of the tablecloth... it seems interesting.* Suddenly, my father sought my attention.

"I found out that you have an interest in attending the school of physical education, right?"

"Yes," I answered quietly with my gaze fixed on the tablecloth. I felt somewhat confused. *Where did this come from? How is it that he knows about my plans?*

"You see, Ernesto, since you find yourself about to finish secondary school, I suggested to your mamá that it would be good if you were to come and live with me."

My father paused, waiting for my answer, but I only nodded my head and he continued with his proposal.

"The school is situated much closer to my house. Your grandmother's house also is in the same direction and she would like to be able to spend time with you. It's been years since she saw you, you know."

I remained speechless. I didn't know what to think; the news fell on my head like a bucket of cold water. *My papá... he lives near the school of physical education and my grandmother...what does she have to do with this? It's been years since she saw me? What is he saying? I don't even know her! What's going on here?!*

"You don't have to decide today. I can return in a couple of days and if you resolve to come with me, you can do it. Ah, of course, you would want to come to spend weekends with your mamá."

After my father left, I angrily asked my mamá, "Do you really agree with this idea? You want me to go back with him?"

She answered me with a great deal of serenity, "Son, calm down a little. Your father and I talked about this. I believe that this is an option for you, especially because of the long commute."

"What? From what I see you have already agreed with him. You want me to rush out of here?" I answered frustrated. I believed at that moment that they were conspiring against me… *My own mother betrayed me!*

"Calm down, Ernestico. Listen to my explanation. I don't want to throw you out of this house; of course, that would never go through my mind. Your father has simply offered you an opportunity to help you with your studies, just to make it easier for you. Whatever your decision is, I will respect it. Nevertheless, I can't deny you the opportunity to live with your father and his family, you know? To make a long story short, they're also your family."

"Yes? Like this when he suddenly shows up? Why?" I said frustrated because I couldn't understand what just happened.

"Understand, Ernesto, my obligation is to advise you. You know that I'll always be here to support you in whatever is offered to you, whatever you decide. The only thing I want is for you to analyze the situation. I believe that, yes, it is a great advantage for you to be near the school, and if at anytime things are not working out, well, so what? You will always have a home here; you'll lose nothing by trying. But right now, eat your dinner and then, with your belly full, talk it over with your pillow."

Of all things to happen to me! Mmmmm... What will I do? It seems suspicious to me that my father, suddenly, just like that, comes to propose that I return to live with him. Why does he want me to return with him? Does he really want to help me with my studies? Is it that he is sorry for the way things happened years ago and wants to mend the past? Or will it be a second chance for both of us? Is it because my grandmother wants to see me too? Confused, I asked myself a thousand questions.

Look before you leap. Be calm, think, analyze well before making a decision... my inner voice advices me.

My mamá is right. I'll definitely be much closer to my father's house while at the university; it's a rather big advantage, I believe. The good thing is that I wouldn't have to leave my mamá completely and this time I doubt that he would dare hit me, now that I am capable of defending myself; he would get into trouble with me. Right then I started to see the situation with more clarity.

After thinking about it for quite awhile, I made the decision to live with my father again. Moreover, I was inspired to return to my sport, kayacking.

***

Now, settled in the house of my father and his wife, I began my studies in the school of athletic training and returned to practicing sports. I adapt easily to my new life style. My father's wife is friendly; I have no problems with her, nor with my father. Practically all day, I find myself outside the house, so I don't spend a lot of time with them.

Just as my father said, I also get to know my paternal grandmother. She's a lovely lady with a nice personality. She doesn't seem that old, even though she is about seventy-five years of age. I try to visit her from time to time and she always receives me graciously. She sometimes will ask me to move heavy things and I don't mind because she happily shares with me a little bread and coffee with milk.

I originally thought that it would not be very entertaining to have conversations with a grandmother; but after a few visits, I found her stories interesting, especially when she describes what life was like before the Revolution and how the dictatorship of General Batista fell. In addition, she seems to be interested in my life, usually asking me about how I'm doing in school and sports.

***

A short while passed since this new stage of my life began. It was during one of my daily visits to my grandmother's house that she asked me if I would like to attend a "quinceañera", or fifteenth birthday party, of the daughter of a friend of the family. Everyone was invited. Without thinking twice, I said yes. *What kind of fool would I be not to go? "Quinceañeras" are always very entertaining, with great food and tons of girls. Since I love dancing, I am sure it'll be great.*

One day before the party, I realized that my schedule was very tight.

"Papá, tomorrow is the quinceañera…right?"

"Yes, and what about it?"

"Well, it's just that…I've got training and I'll probably arrive a little late."

"What? Are you thinking about not going?"

"No, I really want to go, but I was thinking if… is it okay for me to meet you in the party room?"

"Yes, of course it's okay Ernesto, we'll see you there."

After training, I left quickly. I arrived at home and took a quick shower, put on black pants with a light blue shirt, and made sure that my clothes were ironed and my black shoes well-polished. I checked in the mirror to see that everything was on right and left as fast as I could for the party. Luckily, the place was just a couple of blocks from home.

The celebration was in a large yellow house with tall arches of white quarried stone adorning the front of the house. It was a typical colonial construction with a tile roof. I found the main door wide open. To me, that was a sign that guests should feel welcomed. Following the noisy chatter of people, I walked down a wide passage. *It is already past seven in the evening, but I don't think that I've missed a lot since the party began.* I arrived at the end of the corridor where the guests were gathered. The patio was grand, located in the center of the house with a concrete floor and high walls, pale yellow in color. Everything was beautifully decorated with garlands of balloons. The tables, for the guests, were placed around the patio and covered with cotton tablecloths and decorated with centerpieces of paper flowers, out of which emerged a balloon that was attached with a ribbon. Everything was hand-made and pale rose in color.

I looked around, searching for my family, but my attention was drawn to the table in the back, the one for the birthday girl. The table was decorated with an arch of balloons and paper flowers that covered its length and width. In the middle of the table, I saw the quinceañera cake. It was a big cake with many layers, adorned with merengue, flowers made of sugar and ribbons… rose-colored, of course. *Mmmm, that looks tasty! It's been a long time since I have had a piece of cake; it makes my mouth water.*

Aha! There's my family, on the left side of the main table. The host announced the waltz for the quinceañera. I stopped to contemplate the "dueña del santo," the birthday girl. She stood up and went to the center of the dance floor, accompanied by her father, who held her proudly on his arm. All the guests stood up and applauded the celebrated young woman. While a Cuban-style waltz began to slowly play, the father invited the timid young "quinceañera" to dance and she, happily accepted.

Her rose-colored dress, princess-style, was decorated with little satin flowers inlaid on the neckline and the wide, gauzy skirt, that seemed to be dancing to the rhythm of the music. *Without doubt, rose is the favorite color of this girl. This day has to be like a dream come true for her.* I believe that all young Cuban girls, in some moment of their lives dream of having a fifteenth birthday celebration. It is a special day in which they feel like a princess in a fairy-tale; it is their great debut into society as young women. *How beautiful is this tradition and how great does that cake look!*

After the first dance, the entrance of her court was announced which was led by the Escort of Honor. He walked elegantly, with his arms folded behind his back, dressed in a black suit and a rose-colored tie that matched the dress of the "quinceañera." After an elegant bow, her father yielded his position to the boy who took her hand. The rest of the court formed a circle around them. The rhythm of the waltz changed and they began a choreographed dance. *How long must they have rehearsed?* I asked myself.

I continued watching all of the well-synchronized movements of the escorts and their partners; all matching in rose colors. The birthday girl stood out among all of them; her dress was fuller and more glamorous, and she was the only one wearing gloves. On her head, she wore a small tiara and her loose black hair, combed into perfect curls, fell on her shoulders. *Without doubt, this day will be unforgettable for the "quinceañera."*

Someone waved to me; it was my grandmother. I passed between the people who continued to gather around to watch the waltz, and approached the table where my father and my stepmother sat, and… *the girl from the aquatic center!*

"Hey, I know you," Yanina said to me with surprise.

I remained standing there, frozen, equally as surprised as she was.

"Oh, uh, yes, yes…"

My father interrupted me, "See, Yanina, it's your brother, Ernesto."

We were stunned by his words.

"What?" we asked at the same time, both astonished.

In that moment, whatever physical attraction I had for Yanina disappeared. *How much more I don't know about my father?! Never would I have imagined that Yanina and I were siblings.*

After receiving the unexpected news, I felt somewhat uncomfortable seated at the same table with Yanina. I didn't know how to behave, so the rest of the afternoon I tried to avoid her by dancing with other girls and talking with some of my friends who came to the party. Nevertheless, I went back to my seat when the dessert is being served. Yanina, almost naturally starts a conversation with me.

"So, you're my other brother."

"What a surprise, isn't it?" I replied, embarrassed.

"Didn't you know that you had a half-sister?"

"No, no idea. Actually, I lived far from my father for years. It's only been a short time since I moved in with him."

"I knew that I had a half-brother but until now I was in the belief that he lived in Guantánamo."

"Oh, no. I lived there a long time ago. I was just a little boy."

***

The conversation between Yanina and I lasted longer than I'd expected. Thanks to our conversation, I understood the real reason why my father came looking for me. It turns out that my step-mother learned through my father that I attended the same aquatic center as my half-sister. She, rightly so, feared that we would fall in love. Therefore, it was Yanina's mamá who was looking for me. Apparently, she and my father had, after their divorce, kept a relationship that was at least somewhat friendly.

Since that time, my relationship with beautiful Yanina from the aquatic center has grown but not in the precise way that I imagined. My sister, Yanina, and I have always had a nice sibling relationship.

Chapter Seven
My Studies

Shortly after establishing a new relationship with my father, I moved to his house. I also enrolled in "the Superior School of Athletic Refinement", or "La Escuela Superior de Perfeccionamiento Atlético." I had the goal of one day becoming a teacher at a technical college.

Since the school had a kayak team, I had no doubt that I would fit in and begin training again. I felt very excited. The competitions arrived and, without problem, I won the school championship in kayaking. Thanks to this achievement, I was chosen to join the national kayaking team. Yes, once again the opportunity was presented to me. Without hesitating, I accepted the offer.

Full of energy and enthusiasm I was enjoying a new phase in my life. Now, with a certain maturity, I outlined new goals. I dreamed of achieving even more.

My daily routine began very early every morning. I got up at a quarter to six in order to arrive on time for my training. I found myself in the water by six each morning, rowing for approximately two hours. After rowing, the activities varied. There were days that I went to the gym to lift weights; on other days, I ran or practiced swimming. After rigorous training, I had a couple of hours free; those hours were occupied by eating and preparing for my classes. School began at exactly one in the afternoon.

In spite of the fact that I had a very busy day, I was given time during the week to visit my grandmother. The school of physical education was near her home. And, of course, I reserved the weekends to be with my mamá.

I continued to see Yanina, my sister, in the aquatic center. My approach to her changed completely. I continued walking with her each time that I could at the bus stop, but then it was with the desire to protect her.

At the beginning of the semester, my academic grades were acceptable enough. Therefore, I finished my first year of studies without major complications. Although I dedicated a lot of time to my training, I also achieved good grades in school. That year I had the opportunity to attend the National Championship of Cuba, representing Havana, much to my satisfaction.

Neverless, before my second year of school started, my luck changed but not for the better.

Unfortunately, that was the year that my school was relocated, far away from Havana, to the city of Boyeros. This was a problem for me because of the long daily commute to school and additionally because the country's economic situation began to get worse.

In 1991, with the collapse of the Soviet Union, the monetary support for Cuba from Russia was suspended. It was then that a severe economic depression commenced, the so-called "Special Period in Time of Peace". I remember that one of the problems that affected the population was the reduction of transportation which now made it difficult to travel to other areas of the country.

The situation between the school, my papá's house and the sports club was like a triangle. Approximately, I traveled nearly one hundred kilometers daily by bus, but when things changed, I went by bicycle. My daily travel by bicycle was some eighty kilometers when I finally figured out how to take shortcuts and cut the distances. There was no other option; we didn't have another way to travel.

After three months, fatigue began to consume me. I was losing weight and energy and I started sleeping in class without realizing it. At times, I didn't eat because I didn't arrive in time at the school cafeteria where they gave us lunch and I was unable to ride to my father's house either. I still belonged to the kayaking team. In general, this began to complicate my life exceedingly. It finally came to the point in which it became almost impossible to continue studying and training at the same time.

***

One weekend, on the way to my mother's home, I started to reflect on my options. *I'm at the top of my sport now, I'm very fast, I am young and I can go very far in kayaking.* Sports are the main thing that goes through my mind at the time.

"Hi, mamá, I'm home! Mmmm, smells great!"

"Hi, Ernesto, come to the table. I prepared rice with fried plantains."

"Thanks, I am so hungry!"

"Sit down; your plate is already on the table. Tell me how your week went."

"Oh!" I breathe deeply, looking down at my hand, distracted. I don't know how to continue this conversation.

"What's going on?" My mamá asks intrigued.

"I have to tell you something, um... ahhh, you know, mamá, I am doing really well in my sport, I made it to the national team, with great guys," I said, hesitating as I try to explain.

"Oh, yes? With great guys? Are you referring to very cool people?" my mamá answers with a playful tone, meanwhile leaving a pitcher of lemon water on the table.

"No, mamá, seriously. Let me explain."

"Okay, tell me what you are trying to say, son," my mamá answers while she sits down to listen closely. I scratch my head, lower my gaze further and try to get to the point.

"You know that they moved the school; now it's too far from me. It makes it very difficult for me; I feel that now I can't do everything. I can't go to school to study and also train, now that I am so far away."

My mamá, suspecting the direction that the conversation will take, sits upright and with determination tells me, "Ernesto, listen very carefully to what I am going to tell you: sports will serve you well while you are young, but an education will sustain you all of your life."

"Yes, mamá, but I have already made the decision. I have to choose between sports and school and I have reached my best times in kayaking."

Then my mamá tells me for the last time, "No, Ernesto, that will not serve you well in the future. You are going to study a career that you'll choose! Even if it is the last thing that I do in this life, you are going to finish school!"

"You don't understand me, mamá. I've already made my decision; I'm not going to continue in school."

At that moment my mamá walks in front of me, leans forward on the table and with a fixed and penetrating look affirms, "Over my dead body. Look, little boy, once and for all get it through your thick skull that you're not going to leave school; sports are not critical to life!"

"But mamá…"

"No buts, Ernesto, you are going to continue in school, end of discussion!"

"No mamá, look—"

At that moment I feel a strong slap on my face that spins me around. My mother, very frustrated, asserts herself, "You are going to do what I tell you. Period!"

The conversation ends. I turn around and go to my room, clenching my teeth while protesting, "It's not fair. Why do I have to do what you want?!" Now I'm not even hungry. I want to slam the door but I am afraid to do it. *What a slap in the face she gave me! My face still burns. But nothing is worse than this overwhelming feeling of powerlessness ...agrrrr!*

***

I refused to quit the sport. For a couple of months, I made a major effort to continue both things. Truly, I tried to persevere and hold onto my dreams but reality was here, it was a fact. I wasn't making progress with kayaking or school. My times were worsening every day and my grades were going down too. So shortly after, I opted to drop sports just as my mamá told me.

In that moment, my dreams ended for me. I was filled with profound sadness and resignation.

I dedicated myself to studying, although not at the one hundred percent that I had planned. Circumstances obligated me to work along with attending school. I did that for four years, until I graduated, at the age of twenty-two.

Chapter Eight

Work

During the period in which I dedicated myself to studying, I continued staying with my father. The economy of the country worsened and, with that, the financial reality of our family. The situation was so hard that we had to come up with ways to make more money in order to survive. What the government gave the families in food rations was not enough to go around. The salaries were so low that they didn't amount to very much.

Each time I arrived at my father's house I noticed that we had more shortages. I felt an obligation to contribute something to the family. As a student, it was near impossible to find a job that would pay me a decent salary. Nevertheless, it was very clear to me that I had to do something.

***

Upon returning from my mother's home, on a Sunday night, I found my papá in the living room drinking coffee.

"Papá, I need to talk with you."

"Ok, I'm listening," he replied without showing much interest.

"I've been thinking about how to bring some more money home."

"Ah, yes? Tell me, what's your plan?" This time he responds with curiosity.

"I'd like to start a business."

"What do you mean by "start a business"? Ernesto, you know that if people decide to start a business here—"

"I already know that it's not permitted, but if one could…" I interrupted.

"The only way to do it is in a clandestine manner. But I'll tell you right now that it's very dangerous," my papá answered seriously. The word "business" was practically prohibited, he knew just how badly things could go. We both did.

"Yes, of course I know it. Nevertheless, we have to take the risk; there is no other option. You know that things are getting worse all the time. What else can we do? Die of hunger?"

***

I debated with my father about starting a business whenever I saw him. I was aware that if we were to start any kind of enterprise, we would risk it all. If for some reason they discovered us, we would go to jail for an indefinite period of time! There was no freedom in Cuba, not any more.

The ration books that the government gave us were getting smaller and the products in the "bodegas," the stores, were becoming scarce; so the people found themselves searching for other ways of survival. We could barely live for a couple of weeks with what we could obtain in the stores.

I remember standing in the large and annoying lines at the stores to pick up the monthly quota of groceries per person which consisted of five eggs, a little more than a pound of chicken, a half-pound of soy meat, a pound of beans, seven pounds of rice, four pounds of sugar, one-half pound of oil, four ounces of coffee and a bag of pasta. The rest of the supplies had to be purchased in the black market; and, of course, at much higher prices than the articles subsidized by the government.

***

"Okay Ernesto, we will plan well, with much care and with as much secrecy as possible."

After some days of carefully thinking about it, I respond to my papá, "Yes, I understand."

"What's your idea?"

"I have noticed that they use many candles in Havana, for example, the 'Santeria' candles, you know... The Way of the Saints."

"What do you know about Santería? From what I remember your mamá doesn't practice it, and me even less!"

"No, wait papá, this has nothing to do with Santería. This business will be about producing candles and selling them to use them in things like Santería. I know that many people use the candles for rituals, and you probably know a bunch of people who actually practice Santería. In fact, you could be in charge of marketing!"

"And then what? You know how to make candles?" asked my papá with interest.

"Yeah, I know how they're made; it's a very simple procedure actually," I answered very self-assured. I had the opportunity as a child to see how candles are made and since then I had learned a few more steps.

"Okay, sounds like an idea. What happens after that?" my papá prods for more information.

"I've also already found out where we can buy paraffin, string and all the other materials. I already have the contacts."

"From what I can see, you're going in the right direction. Okay Ernesto, let's do a couple of experiments first; and if it works, then we will clear the little junk room on the patio and work there. That being said, no one ought to know what are we going to do, absolutely no one, not even your shadow, understand?"

"Yes, papá, I understand."

After our conversation, I became very confident but remained cautious.

***

Finally, we decided to begin the candle business.

We knew that to get the material we had to buy it on the black market, from other people like us who had a clandestine business. There was no other option. It was a time in which all of us were fighting to survive.

In the matchstick factory, we successfully got the paraffin for wholesale. They sold it to us in sacks, weighing eighty kilos each. This was also where we purchased the string, old pots and molds.

My routine changed when we opened "the business". I woke up early each morning and would start my day in our makeshift factory that we created in the little room on the patio. Afterwards, I went to bathe, get dressed and eat breakfast in order to go straight to school. After returning home from school, I would continue with the candle making process until late into the evening.

At first, our makeshift factory didn't produce much. I remember that in a working day of approximately ten hours, the only thing that came out was about four hundred candles. I began to feel stressed out, in addition to being tired. The hours of work were building up without an opportunity to rest.

*****

One day, standing in the middle of the factory, I paused to think a little. *We have a good market, but not enough time. This entire process is too slow. My father assured me that if we have a way to sell more candles... I have to analyze it... mmm...what do I do? The main problem is the pace. What I'm doing isn't efficient, it takes too much time. Ah! I'm at the end of my rope. At times I feel like I'm at the point of exploding, but I can control myself.*

What can I do to improve this process? I asked myself. *I need to do it much faster.*

I continued studying the technique and procedure that we used to make the candles. Suddenly, I began to understand in detail the manner in which we produced the candles and finally an idea began to form in my head. *Ah! How could it be that this did not occur to me before?*

***

During the next couple of days, I focused on searching for a way of making the process we had for the production of candles more efficient. I successfully increased the production of our factory with a few inventions and modifications that I made to the process.

From four hundred candles that we made per day, we now successfully fabricated up to three or four thousand candles per day. This represented to me a good deal of success. I knew immediately that our life was beginning to turn around. The well-being of our family would once again be restored.

And so it went. In spite of the fact that the country went from bad to worse, money began to come in. In my father's home we now lived more comfortably, we had food and clothing. In fact, during that time in which we successfully increased the production, we never lacked anything.

My father bought a motorcycle, and then sold the motorcycle in order to get himself a car. And although it was an old car, it still was, of course, a luxury in Cuba.

People began to gossip. Inevitably, suspicions arose.

***

One morning, just before the time to leave for school, the doorbell rang. I was alone at home. *Who could it be at this hour?* I opened the door while holding my school books. It was an agent from the National Revolutionary Police. He was a fat man, dark-skinned, he had a moustache and was wearing his dark-blue uniform. He informed me that he had an order to search the house. Although I was very surprised by his presence, I could obviously guess why he came to our house. *Oh, no!*

My heart begun to beat rapidly, but I controlled myself, trying to hide my nervousness. I felt a knot forming in my stomach. *Easy Ernesto, everything will come out okay, just act naturally,* my inner voice told me. Therefore, after recovering from my first impression at the door, I invited him to enter, pretending to know nothing.

"Come in, officer. Allow me to put my books on the table; I was just leaving for school." I gave him a little explanation to try to hurry him up. Nevertheless, the policeman ignored my comments and entered the house walking slowly, with caution. First, he went to the kitchen, opened a couple of cabinets, looked around and found nothing more than pots, old kitchen utensils and a half-stocked cupboard.

The presence of this man made me very tense. He immediately went to the bedrooms and in the same way opened a few closets. He found nothing of value and nothing outside of the normal. Following behind him, I prayed to God that he didn't ask me to go out to the patio. He turned around and asked me what's behind the door at the end of the hallway. I told him that it was the house's bathroom. He walked in that direction, opened the door and leaned his head in to confirm that it really was just a small bathroom. After asking me a couple of routine questions, very solemnly he told me that he had ended his visit and then he left.

As soon as I closed the door, I carefully slid the window curtain back to peek outside to be sure that he left. I watched him get into his car and speed away. When he disappeared from my view, I felt like I could breathe again. *What a relief! How scary! If they caught us... Oh no, I don't want to even think about it!*

***

I was bringing money to our home, contributing to improving the level of my family's lifestyle. However, I had just enough to live. I began to dream about something more. I desired to progress, to eat better, dress better, and to be able to save a little money. Now I wasn't satisfied with the mere act of subsisting.

My aspirations grew and I didn't feel totally satisfied working with my father. He was in charge of administration and made the business decisions while my task was only to make the candles. As time went by, I begun to feel tied down to him.

With similar temperaments, my father and I begun to have disagreements; but I had to be respectful because I lived in his home. I only concerned myself with following the rules of the house and following his orders.

***

Some weeks passed and one afternoon, upon coming home from school, I saw one of those white police cars stationed in front of the house again. *Oh, no! The officer came back!* When I rushed into the house, the first thing I saw was the open patio door. *This time he's going to search the patio!* Shaken, I moved in that direction but stopped when I saw my father walking with the agent. *They are doing business!* I begin to sweat from nervousness. I managed to see my step-mother from the patio door. She was in the kitchen, standing in front of the sink, washing dishes. Without moving from there, almost petrified, she looked at me worriedly; not a word was spoken between us. My father opened the junk room. He stayed outside while the officer entered to search. The officer came out almost immediately.

My father again directed the officer through the house. My father ignored me when they walked past my side. I understood his behavior as a message not to approach them. *It is better to not even run any risk. To initiate a conversation with me could open the door to suspicion.*

Upon seeing my father's calm face, and the same with my stepmother, I realized that all was good.

"The policeman came back! What happened?" I nervously asked my father as soon as the agent left and closed the door.

"Everything is okay; I don't think that he'll return," he replied calmly.

"Do you really believe that? How can you be so sure?" my stepmother interrupted.

"This time he was convinced that nothing is happening here. Everything is okay, calm down," my father assured her.

***

After that second visit from the police, to improve security we constructed a false wall in the little room where we worked; we even hung an old and dusty picture there. Behind this "wall" we hid the materials that we used to make the candles, together with the pots and the rest of the supplies. To give the appearance that this place was really just a small storeroom, we strategically placed various old things in front of it, like a rusted chair, a bicycle that had fallen to pieces, brooms and dirty rags.

Each time that I ended my work for the day, I was in charge of leaving everything hidden behind the wall, and organizing the place in such a manner that it would appear to be a simple junk room.

That time we were lucky, but next time... perhaps not.

Chapter Nine
My Independence

It was a dream come true for my mother when I graduated from school and was ready to embark on a professional career. To please my mother, I accepted everything she said to me. I wasn't able to deprive her of the satisfaction that she felt.

"Ernesto, son, you know that I want to throw you a party for your graduation, right?" my mamá, very happy and motivated, said to me.

"Yes, mamá, it's fine, do as you wish."

I knew that for a long time my mother was saving some money for the day I graduated. Even when I wasn't totally convinced about the idea of having a party, I didn't have the courage to take away the illusion of celebrating that event.

"I am going to plan a grand party here at home. I want to invite your friends, the family, and all of the kids in the neighborhood," said my mamá, bursting with enthusiasm.

She actually went ahead and planned it. She did not organize anything glamorous but the important thing was that my friends and my family were there with us to celebrate the occasion.

My mamá took responsibility for cooking enough food for everyone. Additionally, she placed a rectangular table in the center of the living room and covered it with an old tablecloth. She placed small plates of food (that was ready to eat) on the table, to accompany the roast suckling pig, home-style, which was spectacular! She also served salad with tomatoes, radishes, yucca, fried plantain chips and, of course, black beans and rice. Just remembering the aroma of the delicious meal that my mamá cooked makes me hungry.

My mamá was splendid. She even prepared two large pitchers, one for fruit punch and the other for mojitos. Plus, she purchased a couple of bottles of rum and added music to liven up the party. I was one of the first to eat; I wanted to make sure to try all of the food that my mother cooked with such wonderful flavors.

During the party, between all the music, food and guests, I met a girl. She would become the great love of my life.

***

I was enjoying a glass of wine while chatting with my friends when I suddenly noticed a young woman. She did not notice that I was watching her while she was serving herself food. I looked her over from top to bottom. My jaw dropped. She wore a tailored brown dress that combined perfectly with her dark complexion and high heels. Her hair, long dark and wavy, fell beautifully on her back. *What a waistline!* Her curvy body had the power to accelerate my heart rate. *Ah, she is an absolutely gorgeous woman!*

I went back to the conversation my friends were having and tried to hide my attraction to her. I felt her pass by my side with her plate full of food, looking for a place to sit down. I couldn't restrain myself; I turned my head to contemplate her once more and she turned at the same time. In that moment, we made eye contact. She smiled at me. My heart stopped beating for an instant and I felt gloriously captivated. I replied to her smile with a little movement of my hand.

I was already falling head over heels for her. Without hesitation, I got a chair and offered it to her:

"Hi, here's a chair."

"Thanks," she said and took a seat.

"I'm Ernesto."

"Hi, Ernesto. Don't you remember me? I'm Yadira, your neighbor."

"Really! I didn't recognize you; you have changed a lot."

It's obvious that the neighbor that I usually saw playing with my sister had become a beautiful woman.

"Congratulations on your graduation," she says politely.

"Oh, thanks. Thanks for coming. And you, when do you graduate?"

"I need a lot for that. In truth, I haven't decided what I want to study yet."

We ended up talking for the better part of the afternoon.

The party ended; my mamá was very content and exhausted at the same time. The pride that she felt wasn't enough to hide her fatigue.

"Ahhhh!" my mamá sighed. She threw herself onto the couch, flinging off her shoes, and in almost an instant, she fell asleep.

I covered her with a sheet and paused to observe her for a moment as I reflected, *How kind is my mamá. All that she does for me is incredible. I won't have a long enough life to thank her.* At that moment, I could finally appreciate all of her struggles. Nothing had been easy for her while raising her children.

After a few days, I still felt satisfied and hopeful. I couldn't erase the image of Yadira from my mind. Since my party, I haven't been able to stop thinking of her.

The graduation dance organized by the school was approaching and I didn't have a date. I decided to ask Yadira to be my date.

One afternoon, I made sure that I was nicely dressed and walked to the apartment where Yadira lived with her mother. Nervously, I knocked on the door and stepped back, keeping my hands in my trouser pockets. Her mamá opened the door and greeted me, asking me to come in.

"Hello, Ernesto. What brings you here?"

"Good afternoon, ma'am, I'm looking for Yadira. I wanted to invite her to my graduation dance."

"Oh, yes. Your mamá told me that you have your dance this week. Yadira! Can you come here please? Ernesto is here."

She left as soon as Yadira appeared.

"How are you, Ernesto?" She said and I felt her sweet voice melted me. *Even her voice bewitches me.*

"I came to see if you would like to come with me to my graduation dance, this Friday night."

"Oh, thanks. I would love to go but I can't," she answers shyly.

"...You have other plans?"

"No, it's that..." she stuttered looking for an answer.

"Is it that you don't want to go with me?" I confronted her.

"No, I really would love to go, but... it's a long story," she stated politely.

"Would you like to walk a little and maybe you can tell me this long story?" I changed my strategy with the intention of trying to figure out why she doesn't want to come to the dance with me.

"Ok, wait here for me; I'm going to get my purse and tell my mamá."

I hope that this doesn't turn out to be a fiasco; perhaps this girl has a broken heart. Or she could be downhearted from a previous relationship. If that's it,

I'm toast, I don't think I have a chance with her. I had various thoughts while I waited for her to return.

That afternoon we walked through the park and discussed a thousand and one things. I learned that the girl wasn't suffering from an amorous deception; in reality she was an unaffected and happy young lady. The lack of a dress was the impediment that made her unable to accompany me. That was a relief for me; there was nothing strange or bad in Yadira's life. I enjoyed her company and the walk. The afternoon went by too quickly, like water between one's fingers.

When I arrived home, I talked with my mamá and she, without having to think much, had the solution for the problem.

"Oh, don't worry about that, son. I can modify one of your sister's dresses so that it can fit her well. Just send her notice that I am coming to take her measurements."

"Really?"

"Yes, of course! It's simple; I can fix it in a day."

The day of the dance arrived. It started with all of the graduates walking to the center of the hall, as they were called out by their names, followed by the applause of the guests. Every graduate held his date's arm. Most came accompanied by their girlfriend but in some other cases, the date was a cousin or some friend.

Once all of us were in the center of the hall, the music started. Yadira took my arm and we proceeded to dance the waltz.

It seemed that Yadira and I were alone in the world; I was lost in that magic moment. My senses sharpened; I could notice her delicate smell and the smoothness of her skin.

Yadira looked like a goddess. With simple makeup and her hair up, she wore the dress that my mother fixed. It fitted her to perfection. An old rose-colored dress, with exposed shoulders and a high collar. It didn't have a low neck-line, so I could only see a little of her skin through the lace. The dress was tailored on top, even making her look more sensuous than she was naturally. Yadira was taller than my sister, so my mother, always thinking, added a fragment of silk cloth of the same color, successfully accentuating her waist. Various layers of organza that fell elegantly to the floor formed the skirt of the dress. That night we danced, talked and enjoyed ourselves with our friends. It was spectacular.

A little time later, I asked Yadira to be my girlfriend. In truth, I was crazy about her; I loved her so much.

Life went by normally and I continued working with my father while going out with my girlfriend. During a quiet little walk through the cathedral plaza, Yadira surprised me:

"I have to talk with you, Ernesto. I wanted to ask you something." She took my hand and invited me to sit on a bench next to her.

"Oh, how serious. What is it that you wanted to ask?" I responded to her playfully, while I admired the beautiful view of the Cathedral of the Virgin Mary of the Immaculate Conception (the complete name of the majestic church).

"It is serious, Ernesto."

"Ok, what's going on?" I returned to the conversation, sensing that there is something important that she wanted to tell me.

"I would like us to spend more time together; you know..."

"What? You want us to see each other more?" Astonished, I interrupted and continued talking, "If I do nothing else but work and see you, I almost can never visit my grandmother. Don't we see each other enough?"

"It's not that. What I am referring to is that... I would like us to live together," she said softly.

For a moment, I was speechless. I needed a few seconds to process what I was hearing.

"Yadira, you know that I love you but I'm not ready for that."

"How can you not be ready? Don't you love me enough to live with me?" She questioned me with her eyes watering, the torrent of tears ready to flow freely.

"I adore you, much more than you can imagine! I love you, not only for what you're asking me, but for so much more! The problem that I have is that the money I earn isn't a lot. I don't have much to offer you yet. I'm working hard for that, in order to offer you something worthwhile. Right now, I don't even have a place for us to live. My father's house isn't a good option. Do you understand me?" I took her by the hand and explained with honesty while tears ran down her cheeks.

"I already spoke with my mamá about this, and she has no problem with us living in the apartment with her. Ernesto, my mamá really loves you and accepts you. She even told me that she could support us financially until you establish yourself. To make a long story short, there are only two of us," she explained to me, wiping her face with her hands.

***

On more than one occasion, the idea of becoming independent had already passed through my mind. So, combined with the conversation I had with Yadira, I decided to take that step without thinking of how young we were or of my uncertain economic future. I was crazy in love with Yadira. For me, that was the only thing that counted.

In addition, I was making a fair amount of money with the candle business or at least from my point of view, there was enough money. Nevertheless, what I received was very little.

We have a lot of work at home and the money is coming in, but my future might not be here... I reflected. *Also, before coming to live with my father, we both arrived at the agreement that I would only live in his house until I finished school.* Then, totally decided, I searched for the right moment to talk with my papá.

***

One Saturday afternoon, my father was having his coffee on the patio of the house.

"Papá, I have to talk with you."

My father slowly placed his coffee cup on the table and frowned at me. I understood that from my tone of voice he knew that I wanted to tell him something serious.

"I'm listening," he replied and shifted in his chair, crossing his arms.

"I wanted to tell you that I am done with this business."

"Why?" He answered, taking a sip of coffee.

"I want to be independent, you know. I have a girlfriend and I want to live with her."

"And?" My father responded with a mocking tone.

"Well, I need you to give me some money to start my own life. I want to start my own business."

"No! I'm not giving you any money. If you go, you go with nothing," he answered loudly and forcefully.

I felt as if a bucket of cold water had dropped on me. I didn't expect that response from my father. My father and my relationship, in those times, was different; I had hoped to count on his support. I didn't want for much, only something to start my own life. Furthermore, I felt that I deserved something for all of my sacrifice, work and improvements that I made to our candle business. How naïve I was!

With my pride injured, I was more ready than ever to leave. I responded calmly in order to avoid arguing with him:

"Ok, fine, I'll be going then."

When I turned my back, he was convinced that whatever he said to me to try to stop me would not matter; I was going to leave. He called me and said, "Wait, come here. You're really going to leave?"

"Yes, I'm going to go; I have two arms and I can fight; I'm going to succeed," I answered confidently.

My father, with a strange look on his face, asked me if I would wait a minute. He went inside the house. Upon returning, he walked toward me, with his arm extended in which he was offering me money. I thanked him as I took the money and without another word, I went back to my room and packed my clothes.

After counting the money, I thought about going back to complain to my father. *But if this isn't enough money, what can I do?* Deeply disappointed and humiliated I left my father's house.

Really, the money he gave me wasn't considered much in Cuba in those days; the only thing that I was able to buy for that amount was a soft drink that I shared with my adored Yadira.

***

In Cuba, education is free. As long as a person is a student, one does not pay a single cent. The government absorbs the cost, but this is only until you finish your studies. There's a type of contract, called a "certificate," that you have to complete after you graduate. This specifies a period of time that you're required to work. In my case, I had to work for at least three years to be able to pay for the cost of my studies.

Therefore, the government then put me to work as a teacher of physical education in a school in the same zone where my mother lived, in the north part of the city. It was also, thankfully, the same zone where I lived with Yadira.

What the government paid me wasn't enough to live on. At that time, in 1993, I earned two dollars and ten cents every two weeks. The money the government paid me was, literally, not worth anything. I couldn't even buy a soft drink with it.

What I did was to try my hand on several small businesses, such as shining shoes, or I went into the outskirts of the city in search of vegetables to bring back to the city to sell. More or less, I was trying to do a little of everything to earn a living.

My salary was so low that I didn't feel I was achieving much for my family. I more or less liked the work itself, although it wasn't always so. Since I didn't have experience teaching, it was very hard in the beginning. I remember that the first day of class I struggled with a very difficult group of third graders. That day was a tremendous mess. Altogether, they assigned me eight groups, four in the third grade and four in the fourth, each group with thirty-five students.

After the bad experience of my first day, and being as naïve as I was back then, I decided it would be best for everyone involved if I resigned. I explained to the director that I had made a mistake in choosing my profession because those kids were terrible! I told him that because I didn't have the teaching experience and had no clue about how to manage the situation with the students, I was giving up.

I was told I wasn't allowed to do that.

That day, after I didn't receive the response I wanted from the director, I returned home frustrated and very annoyed.

A few days later, the government made me return to the school because I had made a promise to the

Revolution. They had given me an education, so now it was my turn to fulfill that promise. If you don't follow through with the government's request, it is as if you spent all that time studying for nothing because they will nullify your degree and even follow you around, pressuring you to pay back the education that you received. It's a debt with the government that you have to comply with.

Forced by the rules of the game, I returned. This time, I asked for suggestions from other teachers in order to learn how to manage the problems with the children. Thanks to the help of my cohorts, the experience improved somewhat and from then on I began to enjoy that job.

The school day was from eight in the morning until four twenty in the afternoon. At school, they gave us a snack at nine in the morning and lunch at noon and three in the afternoon they gave us a second snack.

Previously, the system in Cuba worked fine but gradually the country was ruined. The devastation occasioned by the collapse of the Soviet Union was more and more obvious with each passing day. The embargo, (commercial, economic and financial), was extended by the United States, so the economy was constantly worsening. The government began a program to ration food even more. Work began to reduce costs as well. The school was able to continue feeding us at the beginning of the so-called 'Special Period in Time of Peace' but later, the school could no longer afford to provide us with meals. We had to bring lunch from our house, but the problem was that none of us had food at home.

Chapter Ten
The Special Period In Time Of Peace

I lived with Yadira now. Her mother, Jacinta, was devoted to hairdressing. Men's hair, women's hair, dying hair, a little bit of everything; she was a very good stylist. She was practically the key to our survival. All of the money that I earned, I gave directly to my mother-in-law, but it was never enough.

***

One day I went to work; it was like any other normal day at work, except that I had not eaten all day, something that had become more and more frequent. *I am tired and ravenous with hunger! And there is nothing to eat at home, absolutely nothing.* I learned this when Jacinta said, "I have nothing to prepare to eat; I don't know what we're going to do. There's nothing to eat, everything has gone bad."

I listened to her patiently and she continued to speak in a hurried tone, "I have seven hundred pesos, but Cuban pesos, which are worthless! I've walked through the entire neighborhood and I found nothing to eat."

"But, okay, even so, did you find anything?" I questioned her in disbelief.

"Trust me, there's nothing!"

"Wait here. I'll go out with my bike, and I promise to bring back some food."

I rushed out of the apartment. I couldn't accept what my mother-in-law had said and I knew that Yadira would return home soon, and she'd be very hungry.

I traveled through the entire city, all of Havana, to every grocery store and market that I knew of and found nothing. Then I bicycled my way to Cojímar, the little neighboring town where I grew up and once there, I went to all of the places where I assumed I might find food, and still nothing. Then I went to another little village and failed again in my search. Neither did I find anything in the bay. *I can't believe this is happening!*

After I ran out of options, I returned home, exhausted, hungry and ashamed. Like they say in Cuba, "like a dog with its tail between its legs."

When I entered the house, I didn't even want to look at Jacinta. I just placed all of the money I took with me back on the table. But my mother-in-law said with sweetness, "Ernesto, I found a little bit of cabbage and I cooked it in water. We can have this for "dinner" and then tomorrow we'll figure out what to do."

***

That soup, if you can call it that, had neither salt, nor oil… nothing! Just cabbage boiled in water. The economic depression that we were living in because of the dissolution of the Soviet Union and the intensification of the North American embargo was more than evident. The government had to compensate, in some way, for the loss of subsidies that they received from the Union of Soviet Socialist Republics. Castro asked us for patience and demanded that we work harder than ever. Public transportation was replaced by bicycles and carts pulled by mules. Consumption of energy was minimized; they even started transmitting television programs that showed the population how to make sandals from dried plantain leaves. Toothpaste, soap and toilet paper became luxury articles. We were living, or to express it more exactly, were suffering during the so-called "Special Period in Time of Peace."

The three of us began to eat in silence. There wasn't much to say; perhaps we didn't have the energy to complain about the situation. Every spoonful that we took was a strike to our soul. That very sad night, all of us breathed with despair and hopelessness in our home.

The lack of provisions was continually worsening and that night was the first time that I went to bed practically without eating.

After dinner, I searched for a place to be alone before going to bed. I closed myself in my room and cried in silence like a little boy. The rage and powerlessness that I felt was enormous.

It's not right, I want to work, struggle and prosper and... simply put, the system, the government, doesn't allow me to do just that. Not me, nor anyone. Hundreds of families were going through the same situation.

Yadira entered in silence and carefully laid down, pressing her head against my chest. I caressed her without saying a word. I found myself filled with destroyed hope.

If I cannot bring a real meal to the table, I can't ask her to marry me. I don't deserve her. What can I offer you if I have my hands tied?

That night I experienced a series of sentiments. I felt profoundly sad, disappointed, frustrated and angry. On the edge of desperation, I declared, *From this day, I firmly propose to myself to leave this country. I don't know how nor how much time it's going to take me, but I'm going to do it. I'm not going to continue being subjugated by this damned government. I have to put an end to this utopia; that's what this stupid socialist model is. I'll do it for me and for my family.*

Chapter Eleven
The Plan

The country was falling apart. It became so ugly and difficult that I only continued teaching for another eight months. I was forced to look for another job but there were no alternatives. I was very fortunate because a short time later, I found a job as a security guard in the tourist zone. In Cuba, people always searched for work in the tourist zone because it provided more money to be able to survive. Upon changing my occupation, my education certificate was automatically canceled. It was as if I had taken my diploma, made it into a ball of paper, and thrown it in the garbage.

As security guard, I worked hard for seventy-two hours and then rested for thirty-six. Unfortunately, the job only lasted about four months in which I was able to earn a small salary. Part of my salary was paid in U.S. dollars and the rest was paid in Cuban pesos. During this time, I had the opportunity to buy food when it was available and although it was never enough, at least it was something that I could take home. Basically, what a person kept busy doing most of the time in Cuba was feeding oneself and getting dressed every day ...driving a car? Impossible! Truthfully, I never imagined that I would be able to have my own automobile.

Later, my salary as a security guard was decreased and then they ultimately closed the business. I now had nothing more to do. I began to run from here to there, taking advantage of friendships in order to find out how to survive and how to leave Cuba. I even swallowed my pride and went in search of my father. I wanted to see if he could, or even would, hire me again in the candle-making business. However, by that time, everything was very scarce and access to raw materials had disappeared. But who was I kidding? Clearly, I wanted to work to make more money but money was no longer useful to purchase food due to no food existing. Every day the government rationed more.

My idea to leave the country grew more firmly. Then, in one of those fate-changing moments, I met a guy who was also crazy about leaving Cuba.

Filled with hope and impatience, we searched for tractor tires to use as inner tubes. We were hoping that the air-filled tires were big enough to allow us to assemble a raft and flee Cuba.

We prepared our escape plan and in a couple of weeks constructed that raft. But as we approached the moment of truth, my partner got scared. He really didn't have enough courage to venture onto the sea. He would change his mind daily, one day telling me that he wanted to go and the next, he would say "no". When I realized that I would not be able to achieve my objective with this guy, I gave up the plan I had with him. The fear that he had was perfectly normal but I couldn't tolerate the fact that he wasn't sure about what he wanted to do. I was only wasting my energy and time.

I devoted myself to looking for someone else with whom to form an alliance. There wasn't much difficulty in finding someone who had the desire to escape. There were many people who wanted to leave Cuba. My problem was finding someone with confidence and courage. Fortunately, I discovered three good childhood friends whith whom I shared my objective.

Once more, I began to assemble another plan. The raft that was constructed with tractor tires as inner tubes would not be sufficiently strong enough to float two men. We created another water craft with foam rubber. Slowly, those three childhood friends started to lose their nerve too. One day they agreed to go, another day they would say "no, we still need more boat parts" and the next day was "maybe". It was always a different story. My anxiety increased day by day, until I successfully convinced them to move ahead and we finally agreed on a date.

***

We arrive at the bay at night; I have already decided that we would get into the water at eleven.

In spite of my great desire to escape, I also feel uneasy, similar to a premonition. I feel the need to meet with a family member to say good-bye.

My friends are completely confused when I tell them that I have to do something before launching into the sea. I'm the most involved person, what's going on? I go in search of my father.

"Papá, I came to say goodbye, I'm sailing out of here," I say to him rushing my words.

"What are you saying?" My being there takes him by surprise.

"As you heard, I came to say goodbye; I don't want to disappear from the map without telling some family member that I'm leaving Cuba."

"What?" He answers genuinely astonished.

"I haven't told anyone in the family, you're the first," I reveal my secret to him.

"But… when is it that you want to do this?"

"Right now! I'll return to the bay soon."

"Wait son, I can go with you," he puts on his shoes and we leave his house quickly.

I return with my father to the bay and my friends are still there. Rattled, one of them asks me, "What's going on, Ernesto? Why is your father here?"

"Shhh…" I raise my hand to avoid being questioned.

My father approaches the raft, walks around and observes it closely.

"No, Ernesto, this is too dangerous," he tells me, truly concerned for my safety.

"I've already decided, we have a plan and we're going to do it. It's a done deal!" I answer with determination.

"You're crazy, Ernesto! Don't you see that this isn't safe?" He stands with his feet firmly planted on the sand, pointing to the raft; his face is filled with worry.

My friends just shift uneasily but don't intervene.

"Papá, we've invested a lot of time and effort into this plan. I'm not asking for your blessing or your permission," I answer irritated.

"It's not about granting you permission. You have to understand that this thing is poorly made. If you go out to sea with it, it would be suicide. You're all going to lose your lives!"

"Ernesto, perhaps your dad is right," one of my friends interrupts.

"Then, I'd prefer to lose my life than to live here like this… it isn't worth being alive!" As I say this, I'm overwhelmed by sadness but I remain firm in my decision. I'm not going to have my arm twisted. The resentment that I had for my father didn't help me understand his reasoning.

Now without much ammunition, my father shrugs his shoulders and with his voice lowered, uses his final argument, "Then, don't do it for me, but for your mother and for Yadira. Don't make this mistake. Look son, I also want to leave this place. Better to give me the chance to see what I can do and so we'll plan it more safely."

"Come on, Ernesto, let's wait and do what your father suggests," my friends insist.

Disarmed, I agree to their petition. We leave the bay; fortunately, no one comes after us.

***

The resentment and rancor that I had for my father began to disappear. It was the first time that I felt true support from him. His concern was undeniable; after all, he was still my father. That situation became an opportunity to reconstruct the broken relationship that I had with my father.

He was as good as his word. Together, we planned our departure; and this time, with his help, it would be foolproof.

My father had saved part of the earnings that he had taken out of the candle business and, generously, he offered to contribute the money to construct a new embarkment. We took the task of going through workshops, factories and other kinds of locations in order to obtain the necessary materials. In one of those sites, we found the roof of a van. Upon seeing it, we knew that with a little imagination and cleverness we would be able to convert it into a boat. We judged that the size was adequate, as was the fiberglass material.

We could now count on the main part of the craft, but that wasn't everything. The reality was that it was only the beginning and there were many other things that we had to consider. The question wasn't only to find a place to store the boat but a storage area that was large enough for it. In addition, it had to be a location where we could work in secrecy. The act alone of planning or trying to escape was a crime. We had to be extra careful with whom we shared our secret. These were dangerous times in which people were desperate to protect themselves and by doing so, willingly sacrificed others. One could absolutely not confide in anyone, not even in someone's mother.

We agreed not to inform the women. We were not going to take them with us because we did not want to risk their lives. Therefore, I never said anything to my mother, my fiancée, or to my mother-in-law. It wasn't easy. Each time I left I had to invent stories to justify my hours of absence.

We spent nearly six or seven months building that boat. It took a long time because we had very little money that we could depend upon. Even though my father had provided for a nice chunk of the cost of the vessel, he had planned to leave some of the money to his wife and my sister, something he never discussed. Therefore, almost all of the money I earned was invested in the boat. This was still not enough which forced us to include five new men in on the project.

I never again saw my childhood friends with whom I had planned the previous trip. They never came back and I don't know what happened to them. It's possible that they are still living in Cuba. They never were as enthusiastic as I was about leaving the country.

Thank goodness for all the earlier time that I had spent in the water and surrounded by boats. I learned to work with resin because it was needed to repair kayaks. I became a key piece in the assembly of the new craft.

We hid our boat and work in the patio of my father's friend. It was well-hidden. The next-door neighbors never figured out that we were putting something together. The most important thing was not to make noise while working on the project there. If anyone became suspicious or if anyone had motivation to denounce you... bam! You were finished. The government would take you as prisoner. If you went to prison, you were simply no longer a citizen of Cuba.

Finally, after months of work, we all gathered before the boat and my father said to us, "We have finished; we can now launch our craft into the water."

The boat was very nice and also safe; both my father and I knew it.

"Yes, so this is it; we have everything we need," I confirmed my father's words and looked with great satisfaction at the product of our effort. We made it so well that we even installed an outboard motor. We had a sail, oars and a rudder. This boat would be our springboard to a better life, toward a life with freedom.

However, we had overlooked one important detail.

"We don't have a compass, Ernesto!" my father said.

"We need to get one," replied one of the guys.

As soon as I heard the word "get" I realized that we had no money left.

"We'll get it somehow. We are already so far into our plan. A compass will not stop our plans", I said with confidence and encouragement.

Chapter Twelve
The Political Situation Of The Country

Two guys came by with an excellent compass.

"What's going on, Ernesto, we heard that you're going around searching for a compass?" One of them approaches me and happily extends his hand to greet me.

"Oh, yes! Yes, we need a compass!" I turn toward the guy shaking his hand in greeting.

"Well, we have one. If you want it, we can sell it to you for two hundred dollars."

"No, come on! That's too much! We don't even have a peso right now; we've already invested everything that we have to..."

Hanging his head low and changing the tone of his voice, the guy interrupts me with another proposition. "Look... In truth... we have the compass... but if you let us go with you, we could mount the compass on the boat." He makes eye contact, raising his eyebrows a little embarrassed.

"Now I understand."

This all transpired right before Cuba's government opened it's borders for all who wanted to leave the country due to the political problems between Cuba and the United States. The disagreements between both countries had always existed but in those times they were even more accentuated. The economic situation in Cuba was so bad that there was a constant flow of people leaving the country illegally. There were more and more who left by boat. Some of the less fortunate did not make it to Florida but the Cubans who did were rescued by the American Coastguard.

In the United States during the nineties, a humanitarian aid organization, "Hermanos al Rescate" or Brothers to the Rescue, existed. It was primarily formed by an aero-squadron of exiled Cubans and other nationalities, such as Argentinians, Peruvians, etc. They all got together and took on the task of rescuing the "balseros" (those who fled on rafts).

The fleeing Cubans became an international news story that was broadcasted through radio and television. Only one in four Cubans safely made it to American territory. It was impossible not to notice such tragedy. The constant news stories covering Cuba pressured the

Cuban government. The tension between both countries grew.

Cuba accused the "Hermanos to the Rescue" of being terrorists when the Cuban Air Armada shot down two Cessna airplanes in which the "Brothers" piloted over the sea in search of people in need; four Americans were killed. Appalled, President Clinton appeared on television demanding a response from the Cuban government.

*And what of the hundreds of Cubans who lost their lives at sea? ...*I asked myself. *Could you not arrive at the conclusion that the government of Cuba also assassinated them?*

I had the impression that the Cuban government felt ridiculed, cornered and obviously very annoyed. These events pressured the Cuban government to open the Cuban ports to all who wanted to emigrate. Those who wanted to attempt to leave Cuba could go by sea. That way, or so I believed, the Cuban authorities attempted to give a lesson to the American government and the "Hermanos al Rescate" organization.

On the other hand, in my opinion, I believed it could have been a strategy that the government used to obtain income. The principal sources of income that Cuba had were tobacco, sugar and tourism. With the economic crisis spreading across the country, resources became scarce, the production of sugar and tobacco were minimal, and we are not even talking about tourism. Cuba found itself submerged in total poverty.

Perhaps that strategy worked well for the government of Cuba. Nowadays, I believe that eighty percent of the money that Cubans live on is sent by their relatives from outside the island who are helping their families.

We wanted to leave the country as soon as possible because we didn't want to run the risk that the government would change the rules, so we accepted the deal with the compass.

By the time we were ready to flee, we were a total of nine people leaving Cuba in one raft.

Chapter Thirteen
The Journey To Freedom

Lying in bed but awake, I observed Yadira sleeping peacefully by my side. I slowly neared her face trying to steal a little of her breath. I wanted to memorize every detail of her profile. I began with her full, perfectly outlined eyebrows, then her nose, straight and turned-up at the end, and her full, rose-colored lips that called out to me like a magnet. I kissed her and she, between dreams, responded with her eyes half-opened but in an instant, she fell asleep again. I caressed her cheeks, naturally blushing with that deep sleep, and combed her hair with my fingers.

"Ernesto, what are you doing? Go to sleep, you need to rest." Although dozing with her eyes closed, she gave me a sleepy smile.

"Okay, Yadira. I only wanted to tell you that I love you," I replied while embracing her delicately.

"I love you too," she answered softly. This time it was she who kissed me and then went back to getting comfortable in her sleep without knowing that in the morning, I would no longer be there.

I got up without making any noise and walked to the kitchen to place a small note on the table.

"Dearest Yadira, you know that lately each day life here has become more difficult. With great sadness I've left Cuba looking for a better future; I'm going by sea in search of freedom. Forgive me for the pain I'm causing you. It wouldn't be fair on my part to ask you to wait for me. But please don't forget that I love you. Yours, Ernesto."

***

The fourth of September, 1994, I leave home with my heart broken at the age of twenty-three. The pain, nevertheless, doesn't blind me from my goal because I'm totally committed. It's two in the morning and I go to the location where I agreed to meet with the rest of the guys. My father is with them.

The night before we arranged to rent a truck large enough to move the raft to Guanaba, a beach on the east of Havana and our place of departure.

Thanks to the authorization that the Cuban government grants us to leave the country, we were able to pack that boat freely. It is so heavy that we need to get the help of twenty-five or thirty men to lift it (we didn't have anything like a tow truck available back then). It is now five in the morning but our craft is already in the water. The moon illuminates the beach with splendor.

We're not alone; there are hundreds of boats ready to depart. I see large numbers of people congregated on the edge of the beach. People are saying goodbye, giving hugs and blessings. I hear the cries of the women, sisters, mothers and wives, all inconsolable. In spite of the beautiful dawn that we experience during this summer aurora borealis, one breathes an atmosphere of sadness and nervousness. I feel great tension and try to divert my attention and focus on the supplies, reviewing that everything is as it should be. While I'm doing that, I hear a broken voice behind me, "Son…"

I turn to find the silhouette of my mother. I stop, astonished. *She's here!* I see her distorted face, with tears in her eyes and reaching her arms out toward me.

"Ay, son, my little boy!" She embraces me with all of her strength.

"Mamá, but what are you doing here?" Confused, I turn sideways and look at my papá with an accusatory gaze.

"I had to do it." My father justifies himself with a shrug of his shoulders.

"No one was supposed to know anything. I was going to send you a message with the sister of a friend."

"Thank God I am here to give you my blessings and to say good bye. I'm not going to complain; things are as they have to be. Please be careful," she says, trembling and gliding her hands by my arms.

"Yes, mamá, don't worry, you'll see it will go well, with God's favor." I try to calm her, knowing that I don't have the certainty that we will come out of this odyssey alive.

"God goes with you and when you arrive at your destination, don't forget that you have your mother here in Cuba. I love you," she says and I hear so much despair in her voice.

"Me, too. But don't be disheartened, you're going to see that when you least expect it, you'll receive a message from me. I'm going to succeed, I assure you."

I feel a knot in my throat and want to fall apart when she hugs me strongly and kisses my cheek but I control myself. I must not show any signs of weakness.

I wait for all of my partners to settle in the boat before getting in myself. As we move away from the shore, in the distance, I hear the cry from my mother, "Ernestico! Take care of yourself!"

I don't turn back. I do not want to take the image of my devastated mother with me.

The boat inches slowly, it seems like the rays of the sun embrace the light of the moon. The hustle and bustle of the beach begins to diminish; little by little we find ourselves almost in silence. Only the sound of the craft and the roar of the sea can be heard. Now I am serene; I commend myself to God.

My God, I place my life in your hands. If by your wish I arrive in the United States, guide my way to honestly reach a worthy life. But if it is not your wish, don't allow me to return alive. I implore you, my God.

***

We have stayed on the coast near Cuba for about four or perhaps five hours. This began to make me worried because I had heard stories about friends who left the country and then immediately said good-bye to the horizon. We, with so much time in the water, and nothing. It was then that I realized what happened. The compass was poorly situated. It wasn't until past ten in the morning that we successfully placed the compass in the right position.

We were lucky because realistically we didn't go in the wrong direction. The error made us go toward the east of Cuba, which helped us position ourselves closer to a straight line towards the United States. It was around one-hundred and forty-five kilometers in distance. Finally, we commenced navigation toward the north.

We followed our new trajectory, and in a matter of an hour and forty minutes, we lost sight of the coast.

***

The guys talk seriously while I am focused on my thoughts of complaining to my father in regards to informing my mother but I resist.

Confronting him isn't worth it. The blessings of my mother that I carry with me are worth more than my ego, as offended as I am by my father. I reflect, feeling certain tranquility for having had the opportunity to say good-bye to my mamá. I closely observe the ocean's turquoise blue color that appears between the waves and rocks us from one side to the other. It brings up pleasant memories from my childhood, when I used to play in the sparkling waters of the river in the village where I grew up.

Suddenly, there is a loud bang. The boat's motor is beginning to give us problems. The craft jerks for a while until, wrapped in a trail of white smoke, it stops completely.

We've lost the motor. We find ourselves forced to row with the oars in order to continue our journey. The conversations between the men die down.

It's noon, yet the darkening sky makes it look as if it were nightfall. The movement of the sea begins to change; now it sways with more energy and its color turns gray. We feel the wind blowing harder. The flashes of lightening, accompanied by loud thunderclaps, illuminate the firmament. Rain begins to hit against the inside of the boat.

Suddenly, the Cuban Coastguard appears at the side of our boat.

One of them turns toward us, yelling with a loudspeaker, "A storm is approaching; you should go back!" My friends turn and look at me as if wanting to ask what we should do. I give them a little hand signal to ask them to remain calm. "I repeat; you should go back! Second call!"

"No, no one here is going to go back!" I stand up and yell at them holding my hands around my mouth.

"The storm is going to worsen!" They advise us.

After a little silence, they begin to come closer and insist, "The storm is going to get very bad; that craft won't survive it!" They warn us.

When I see that they're coming closer and closer with every passing second, I raise my voice with exasperation, "If you want to kill us, or perhaps sink us, do it! Do what you have to do! We are going ahead in peace! But don't get any closer because then there is going to be a confrontation; we're ready to fight!"

"We're only trying to save your lives."

Then the boat moves away. I breathe a little more easily, but not for long.

The weather worsens, the wind blows harder, the rain falls with greater intensity and the skies don't stop shuddering. I grew up by the sea and I'm not afraid. I know perfectly well that there's nothing that we can do, just hold on tightly to the oars and pray.

The sea roars without stopping, our boat seems to have been converted into a pathetic child's sheet of paper that floats in the middle of the ocean. The waves are truly ferocious, making the boat violently rock from one side to the other, tossing our bodies around and striking our faces. It is difficult to breathe. Half of the men are scared, trembling. Some are even crying, terrified.

The fear on the boat grows.

These strong and sturdy men are terrified. Most of them are mentally and physically exhausted. They are panicked about dying and have transformed into nothing but used rags. They're completely drained, it's like they've lost hope.

It is in this moment that I learn to understand men. On land, tall men with large muscles appear as if they are strong and brave. Previously, I assumed that those well-built men would have the same desire to live and go forward as I felt. I now know that this is not true. Many of those strong men will lose their temper and become defeated in difficult situations like this one.

Thank God that my father, although being the oldest crewmember, is not one of those men who are easily knocked down. In spite of being physically depleted, he never stops fighting. His fortitude allows me to remain strong in order to be able to help the others.

God, protect us, we are in Your hands! I entrust myself once again to God.

After hours of terror, the storm stops. I'm exhausted. It is as if the ferocious sea had sucked away all of my energy.

We continue, surrounded by water, everything remains blue; in whichever direction I look everything is just… blue. The water and the sky, both colored blue, fuse at the horizon.

The sun is now incandescent, with no more clouds in the sky. One could no longer hear the clamor of the storm. Now there is vomiting and groaning from the men.

Even though the fatigue is extraordinary, four of us continue rowing. Every time I move the oars, it represents a step toward freedom. I think of the days of hunger and desperation when I lived in Cuba, of the long walks traveling day after day to find food and of the working days without being paid. Courage returns to me and I raise my head and try to concentrate on my goal, on my dream.

After a short while there are more men vomiting. I also feel nauseated; my stomach begins to turn. I've barely straighten myself when one of the guys speaks up, "It's better to turn around; we can't continue like this, we don't want to."

"Turn around?" I reply furiously. The hunger and unbearable thirst that I feel will not stop me from reasoning.

"Yes, I said that it'll be better to turn around," my friend insists.

"Listen well. Some of you would like to have many things in this moment. You can wish for whatever you want but this boat isn't going to turn around, it's going to continue going forward," I answer exasperated.

I have no more patience. It's too late to turn back. I don't understand how such an idea occurred to this guy. *After all of our gains going forward, this guy has to be delirious!*

"Okay, then let's fill the inner tubes. We can go back in them," insists the pigheaded one.

"But what are you saying? No way! The inner tubes remain in their place!" I ordered them. "If another coastguardsman appears, then you can go but meanwhile, no one is going anywhere."

I'm glad I convinced him. I knew we couldn't release the inner tubes just like that. They were our survival plan "B" in the extreme case of being shipwrecked.

***

Finally, I was able to calm him and without any more discussion, we continued our voyage.

Knowing that in Cuba there was nothing more left, I told myself that I must remain firm. There were no other options than to maintain my position and be unrelenting to those who wanted to desert our journey.

**

We spent about ten hours navigating when I noticed Alex, a close friend since infancy who I always respected. Alex was quietly seated with a fixed gaze toward the horizon. I watched him for a long time; he was squatting down without moving or changing his position.

"Hey, Alex," I addressed him but he ignored me completely.

"Alex?" I tried again while I continued rowing but there was no response. A little worried, I started to remember hearing people say that in this type of situations people can suffer hallucinations or get sick or even go crazy.

"Alex, are you okay?"

Without turning around to look at me he extended his arm backward and signals me with his hand, as if letting me know that he didn't want to be bothered.

But, what's going on? This kid worries me; his behavior is troubling. This guy isn't the Alex that I know. In spite of his younger age, during all this time Alex has been one of the few men who has remained calm.

Is he really going crazy? He has been sitting there a long time in the same position, perhaps for an hour! And he seems so lost in thought.

"Alex, are you feeling okay? What's going on, kid?" I insisted.

"They are coming, Ernestico," he finally answered.

I handed my oar to the man next to me and drew near Alex with curiosity.

"What's going on?" I asked, intrigued.

"Look there, look right ahead of us, and tell me if you see something."

"Alex, I don't see anything," I answered while trying to see what he was talking about.

"No, Ernesto, you really don't see anything?" he replied, a little surprised.

"No, Alex, but stay calm and I'm going to continue rowing."

This guy really has gone crazy! Now I am really worried about him.

I rowed and looked at Alex. He was a scrawny little black kid; in truth, the only one that appeared to be weak out of my friends but he always had a very strong and positive mind. It was for this reason that we decided to take him with us.

"Ernestico, come now, and look there!" He excitedly calls me back.

I again let go of my oar and observed the distance. I was able to detect a little white point. I could see it very far in the distance, almost at the edge of the horizon where one loses sight of the sea in the sky.

"Yes, Alex, it seems that there's something there."

After a few minutes, we became aware that a boat was nearing us little by little; the closer it came to us, the better we were able to make out the craft.

What impressive eyesight you have, Alex! How did you successfully notice that ship so far away? Thinking over and over to myself, quietly surprised.

The closer the ship sailed, the men became more happy. Finally! It was an injection of hope. All of us could breathe a little more easily.

It was now about four in the afternoon and we continued rowing with renewed energy. We were advancing rapidly with the help of the wind. We were, perhaps, about one hundred kilometers north of Cuba.

We continued navigating at that speed for more than an hour. We could now see a boat near us; I calculated that it couldn't be more than two or three kilometers of distance from our craft. We were sufficiently close to that boat and we could see all of its details. It was a white boat with a red stripe; it looked like one of Cuba's coastguard boats but it wasn't.

"They're American coastguards!" I confirmed.

"We're saved! We've done it!" One of them yells filled with joy. A few of my friends could not stop shouting. Now with confidence that we would be rescued, we desperately drank the rest of the water that we have stored.

In the blink of an eye, hundreds of rafts appeared. It was incredible to see all those boats suddenly appearing from nowhere. There were a hundred or maybe even two hundred! I believe that all of them also used the American coastguard boat as their point of reference.

One American lifeboat patrols between all of the "balseros", or rafters. Their priority is to identify the people that are in poor health. In spite of the wear and tear that we feel, the Coastguard asks us to wait and witness the other Cuban boaters' despair and misery. Helpless bodies are transported by the coastguardsmen. We were in the middle of a nightmare. We could hear the cries and groans of those gravely affected or close to dying. The pain of the families of others who have lost their lives in search of freedom was very evident. I could feel the tears openly running down my cheeks.

What crime have we committed? The dream of freedom! These are your people, Fidel! Those who you have let down! May God forgive your cruelty!

Chapter Fourteen
Guantánamo

At nearly six in the afternoon, we set foot on an American boat. I'm hungry, thirsty and depressed. We walk along a corridor, escorted by various coastguards or American Marines; honestly, I don't know what position, rank or charge they have. Without any explanation, they ask us to enter a small room. It is filled with people! I have barely begun to acclimate to the situation when I hear a shout followed by a shove, "Just another Cuban!"

What is this? Just another Cuban? This space is so crowded; we're about five hundred people! I turned around and try to take in the situation.

We are in a standing-room-only type of situation, like caged animals, inches from one another without being able to move.

Standing and being watched closely by the American guards' time went by: one, two, three, four, five hours …and there we stood, breathing each other's air. Six, seven, eight hours …we continue in the same position. My legs tremble, everything begins to hurt: my back, my head, my stomach. It is so hard to breathe! Fifteen, eighteen, twenty hours! My anxiety shoots up, desperation takes over. I feel terrified now!

My God, what is this? This is Hell! When I believed that I had lived the worst, I was wrong. Just another Cuban! Is that all that I am to them? Just another Cuban! They want to say just another animal! What have I been reduced to? To a wild beast, to nothing!

There, with the American coastguard, I survive the longest and darkest twenty-four hours of my life. I have no words to describe how I feel during all of this time; it is mental and physical torture. Compassion for man, and respect for life do not exist here; I feel like I am living in a world of misery and pain.

Where's the principal of equality, stipulated in the Universal Declaration of Human Rights? Doesn't it perhaps say, "All human beings are born free and equal with dignity and rights." It's more than obvious that all of that doesn't exist here; we're nothing to them.

The following day, they take all the exhausted Cubans to an American Navy warship. *What an immense thing! It's incredible how huge this ship is. It may be able to carry five-thousand people.* I am finally allowed to use the bathroom for the first time in more than twenty-four hours. I'm thankful to have permission to urinate, as incredible as that seems. I repeat, I'm thankful because they have granted me authorization to do something as natural as urinate. Water and granola bars are all the food that we get to eat during the time that we're on that ship.

Six days later, we arrive at the naval base of the Americans in Guantánamo. I'll always remember that unmistakable voice of a Puerto Rican who tells us through a loudspeaker, "You'll never travel to the United States! You'll never get into the United States! You're only going to be here temporarily, as refugees of sorts, until we can send you back to where you came from!" He tries to discourage us.

When I disembark the ship, I sink five inches into the ground. I look down and see that my shoes are covered in a dust that goes from a white to a dark coffee color.

Looking up, I can see a new view. The camp where they'll place us sits in a huge plot of land. It's fenced and filled with tents. We're confined to this place, with nearly twenty-five thousand other Cubans.

***

They assigned me a cot; it was there that I lived through long nights of sadness. No one offered us any type of encouragement.

Once again, I began to experience a lack of the basics that, in my opinion, one needs in order to live with dignity. I was poorly dressed, filthy and incessantly hungry. In the beginning the meals were small in the refugee camp and even the water was insufficient. Taking a shower was some sort of luxury.

After several months of living in those circumstances, the greatest doubts creeped upon me. *Was it worth to leave Cuba? To leave my loved ones?* I shook those doubts off because at least we had something to eat. The Coastguard began feeding us the same food packets used by the United States military.

The first months were dark. I felt worse than imprisoned. I was so depressed that I was sure that I was going to give up but then mail service became available to us. I could write to Cuba! My mamá, my sister and even my mother-in-law began to write to me. Every time I received a letter, there was encouragement.

I did not receive any letters from Yadira, yet I continuously wrote her. Finally, I received a letter from her. Her response became my driving force of hope to continue.

A few months later, the situation improved. They made a dining room where they now gave us hot meals. There were approximately thirty-thousand refugees. We became some sort of community. As the Americans implemented various occupational activities, I chose to take classes in English and computing. Although I didn't learn much, I tried to keep myself occupied.

The future was uncertain. In that place, we never received any type of hope. Many of my friends began to defect. At that time, it was just a question of going to the border, telling them that you wanted to return and then they'd opened the doors. However, I never lost faith. I decided to bear down for as long as what was necessary. Returning to Cuba wasn't an option for me; that was not an alternative after everything that I had suffered through.

Eight months in, I became accustomed to that place. The soldiers offered me work as a carpenter, helping with the construction of houses near the base. They didn't pay me but in addition to having the privilege of being able to leave and enter the camp, while working I was able to collect scraps of wood and other materials to make handmade crafts. I searched for glass bottles, small pieces of wood and whatever else that was available from the carpenter's workshop. I cleaned the glass bottles and created little sailboats in the bottles with my found materials. They were beautiful. I began to make a living from selling these handmade crafts.

The fact that I could enter and leave the camp gave me a sense of freedom that helped me emotionally feel that I hadn't lost my dignity as a man. It seems incredible but many Cubans tried to enter Guantánamo illegally; they would throw themselves into water infested with sharks to be able to enter the camp across the sea. In those attempts, many of them were maimed or lost their lives.

In that stage of my life, I learned that a human being adapts to all environments and conditions. I tried to invent ways to make life a little more satisfactory: I took up exercise, ran a lot, and lifted weights. We thought up things to do with concrete and sticks; at night we played cards, dominoes, and made wine with the fruit that they gave us.

After a year in Guantánamo, I was convinced that I would remain there forever but news began to arrive. The Cuban community of Florida, which had many relatives in Guantánamo, realized that nothing was being accomplished. The Cuban community began to demand that President Clinton take notice of our situation. Political pressure grew constantly and the monetary cost that represented our maintenance was very high for the U.S. government; the international image of the United States appeared to be worsening.

Due to the mass exodus of Cubans in 1994 (known as the "Crisis de los Balseros" or the Crisis of the Rafters) and because of political pressure, both countries signed migration agreements in which the United States government promised to give out twenty-thousand visas annually to Cuban citizens and to repatriate those illegals intercepted on the sea. Cuba, for its part, assumed the responsibility of accepting those repatriated and for passively allowing people to flee illegally.

Thanks to those agreements, the policy we know today as "dry feet, wet feet" was born in the United States. It calls for the United States authorities to accept those who touch ground in the mainland and return those intercepted on the sea.

***

Finally, they approved the law that will permit us to travel to the United States.

After fourteen months and fifteen days of miserable life in Guantánamo, I leave for the United States.

They transport us in a military airplane. *Never in my life did I imagine I would fly in an airplane. How great is this!* Now seated on board the carrier, I try not to think too much. I concentrate on the noise that comes from the plane turbines and how we begin to move rapidly until we take off.

On October 16, 1995, we land in the military base at Homestead, Florida. After exiting the tail of the airplane, the first thing I do is kneel down, kiss the ground and give thanks to God.

Immigration processes me. They move me to Memphis, Tennessee because I have no family in Florida. The majority of cuban refugees in Miami are the refugees who already have relatives who live there. In fact, presently there's a large Cuban community there and the streets of Miami are flooded with the taste of the island.

A man comes to pick me up at the airport. He introduces himself as a member of a church.

"Good afternoon, welcome to Memphis. My name is Martín," the man greets me.

"Thank you, good afternoon," I say, shaking his hand.

"Follow me; we're going to go to my car." Gesturing with a friendly sign, he shows me the way. We get into his car which seems very modern to me. Again, I never thought that I would ever ride in such a nice automobile. It is white with electric windows and even has interior climate control!

"Our church, "Charity Church", is going to take care of your housing needs for the time being," he explains while we drive.

"Thanks," I answer while admiring all that I see around me. Everything looks different: the automobiles, the streets, the buildings and the vegetation.

"Yeah, it's a nice little apartment that I think you can really get yourself established in. But first, let's stop and buy something to eat," he explains to me. I listen attentively, feeling very grateful.

We stop in a supermarket. I feel very cold and began to tremble when we exit the car. I shrug my shoulders and cross my arms, trying to warm myself as we walk. The shorts that I'm wearing are not appropriate for the climate of Memphis.

I am surprised to see that the grocery store's door opens by itself, as if by magic! I enter the store and I can't believe what I'm seeing. I'm amazed. I turn around and say to myself, *What a strange thing, there is food everywhere; I've never seen anything like this. Definitely, these stores are very different from the Cuban ones. This is a world of food!* I continue looking around and explore all corners. Everywhere I turn, there are different types of food: boxes, cans, fruits, vegetables, and all kinds of meat and fish! *This must be a dream! It is my dream made into reality!*

We leave there and then I can see clearly everything that surrounds me. The impact of what has happened finally presents itself. *How many of those fleeing, who entered the sea in search of freedom, lost their lives in that difficult journey?* Images of the darkest moments of my life cross my mind. Then, grateful, I kneel and turn my face toward the sky and without fear, I cry, "Finally I have my blessed freedom! I am going to work hard, I am going to try hard, and I am going to succeed! Thank you for this new opportunity."

Silvia C. Rodríguez

Contents

www.ingramcontent.com/pod-product-compliance
Lightning Source LLC
Chambersburg PA
CBHW030343180626
46812CB00007B/2744